AUCTIONS AND ALIBIS

CAPE HOPE MYSTERIES

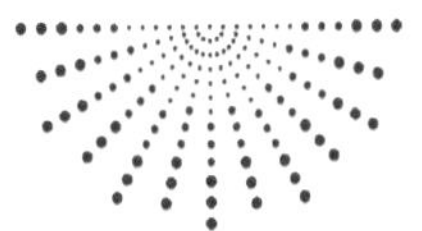

WINNIE REED

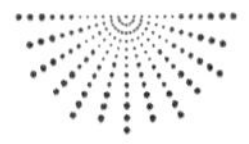

"It looks like we're in good shape even with the off-season hitting us." Becca scrolled through the reports she somehow magically generated and pulled up on her tablet for the purpose of what I'd imagined would be a casual sort of meeting. I'd invited my assistant out for pizza and wine in the hopes of catching up after weeks of my being rather absent from the bookstore.

I should've known better by now. The girl took business seriously.

Not that I didn't. It was my store, after all. *First Edition* was the thing I was most proud of. My baby—corny, but true.

But my assistant took things to the next level time and again. To the point where I wondered how much revenue I'd left on the table for years before hiring her. I could've raked in the dough if I'd implemented her ideas sooner.

To say nothing of the work she took off my shoulders.

She was so good, in fact, that when a friend of mine needed help with her florist shop while her assistant went out of town for a family emergency, I'd been in a position to offer my help. A big funeral had been set to take place, leaving Olivia in need of a spare pair of hands to get everything arranged and delivered to the cemetery.

Silly me, not guessing a simple gesture of goodwill might lead to a near-death experience. To say I'd been distracted recently by the mystery surrounding Pierce Cornell, Emily Newberg, and the entire sordid family would've been an understatement.

Hence the dinner meeting with Becca. I needed to get my head in the game.

I leaned across the table to grab a second slice of hot, cheesy goodness while mulling over the figures Becca had just presented. "You're so much better at this than I am."

"That's not true. We have differing strengths, is all."

I could see her point, even if she was being way too modest.

"I'd like to come up with ideas to bring in more foot traffic. Don't get me wrong, doing business through the site is a huge deal. It's keeping us in the black. But I don't want to forget bringing the community together when we can." Otherwise, as far as I was concerned, nothing was separating us from a big-name online retailer. Sure, I appreciated the convenience of being able to order just about anything online, but there was no ridding me of my small-town-girl mentality.

"I'm sure we can come up with all sorts of ideas. What about another Restaurant Week? I thought we were trying to work something out with the business association."

"Mom was on that for a little while, but the calendar's pretty full through the end of the year. Winter's a little bit of a gamble, weather-wise, if we're looking to attract customers from the tri-state area."

"I guess that makes sense." She tapped her chin while gazing out the window. I knew better than to interrupt her when she was deep in thought, so I turned my attention to dinner. Angelo's pizza was some of my favorite in town, which was saying something, considering the number of parlors on the boardwalk. Everybody had their favorite and, like people tended to do when there were absolutely no real stakes involved, they were willing to throw down in defense of its honor.

Me? I was only sorry my sister and her husband had recently moved to a bigger apartment to prepare for the arrival of their first baby. Not that I'd ever begrudge the baby a room of their own or anything like that, but now I didn't have as many excuses to "swing by" the pizza shop on my way upstairs to Emma's.

Becca's hand slapped the table hard enough to make me jump. "What is it?" I expected a revelation, some magic recipe for endless success.

Instead, the girl looked like she'd seen a ghost. "You've got to be kidding me. What's he doing here?"

"Huh?" I looked out onto the street and instantly dropped my slice in favor of picking up a napkin and wiping my mouth. Of all times for Ethan Crosby to come strolling along—and it looked like he was on his way inside.

"Why would he be here?" I realized Becca was just as shaken up as me, which struck me as odd considering I was the one Ethan had asked to dinner. Unless there was something I didn't know about them? No, that was silly. Was it?

"Why wouldn't he be? He lives here."

Becca turned to me. "What are you talking about?"

"What are you talking about?" I looked out again and finally noticed Ethan wasn't alone. I was too busy freaking out over his approach to notice the guy walking with him. He was cute, with Ethan's dark coloring and lean frame.

Obviously, Becca knew him. I couldn't wait to find out how, since she was generally closed-lipped about her private life.

Ethan stopped short at the sight of me. I wasn't imagining things, either. He flat-out froze, staring at me like a deer caught in headlights. It took a lot for Mr. Unflappable to break like that.

"Hi." I even wiggled my fingers like a complete dork. The man asked me to dinner, and I'd turned into a goofy, nervous pre-teen.

"Hey." It was a grunt, but then that was one of his preferred methods of communication. Right up there with smirks.

Becca stunned me by jumping up from her chair and going to Ethan's friend with one arm outstretched. "You're Max Greene, aren't you? I am such a fan. I've read all of your books and attended the signing you did in Paradise City back in April."

Wow. Even Ethan looked surprised.

Max, however, did not. His smile almost blinded me when he turned it on Becca, taking her hand in both of his. "Guilty. And what's your name? Sorry, there were a lot of readers at the signing, and I've always been terrible with faces."

What a charmer. I glanced at Ethan, who openly rolled his eyes and looked generally disgusted.

"My name's Becca." The girl giggled. She actually, literally giggled, as if her name was funny all of a sudden. "I work at a bookstore here in Cape Hope. *First Edition*. You should drop by while you're in town."

Whoa, Nellie. Time to rope this in. "Hey there, save some for the rest of us." I extended my hand with a sheepish smile. "Darcy Harmon. Owner of *First Edition*. It's a pleasure to meet you." I'd heard his name before and knew he was a recent addition to the *New York Times* bestseller list.

I glanced Ethan's way and found him just as unimpressed as before. "Ethan, I had no idea you spent time with talented authors. You've never so much as bought a book from my store."

"My cousin has good taste in books. Like mine, for instance." Another megawatt smile from Max. So they were cousins. That explained the somewhat similar looks, not to mention the fact that they were together at all. Ethan had never struck me as someone who suffered company unless it was absolutely necessary.

Ethan jammed his fists into his pockets while

rocking back and forth from his heels to the balls of his feet. "Anyway, I made the mistake of thinking I was hungry and suggested we grab something here. Stupid me."

"Why don't you join us?" Becca was firing on all cylinders. "We were wrapping up a strategy meeting for the store. You know, your last book practically flew off the shelves."

"It did? I'm thrilled to hear it." Becca gestured toward one of the empty chairs at our table and Max took a seat.

"I guess the meeting really is over." I turned to Ethan, who was as perplexed as me.

"I'll order us a pie." Ethan's words fell on deaf ears, since Becca had already latched onto Max and was now pumping him for information on his next book.

I leaned in a little. "I'm sorry."

"Don't be. Nothing to be sorry for." Our eyes met for a heartbeat before he looked toward the counter. "Guess I'd better order if there's any hope of eating tonight. It seems like my cousin's too busy flirting with Becca to remember why we came in."

"Wow. You're even worse than your usual level of grumpy. What's going on?" I kept an eye on our table in case Becca decided to offer Max a paid residency at the store or something like that.

He shot an exasperated look in that direction, too, where his cousin laughed at something Becca said and Becca giggled again. I was starting to look forward to the merciless teasing she deserved. "He's always like this. When we hang out, just the two of us, he's a normal person. My stupid cousin who used to wet the bed every time he spent the night."

"Did he really?"

"Until he was eleven." He raised an eyebrow. "Don't you dare think about it."

"Oh, come on. I'm insulted you'd even imagine me mentioning it."

"You're right. Sorry." He rubbed the back of his neck, grimacing. "When he puts on the aw, shucks act it makes my skin crawl."

"You run into his fans on the regular?"

"He has a habit of suggesting we hang out where his fans might happen to be. Like when he has a signing in Paradise City and asks if I want to swing through and say hi."

"Ooh, were you there when Becca was? She never mentioned seeing you."

"Yeah, well…" He scowled, sliding me a guilty look. "I might've avoided her. No offense to her or anything."

"I get it. You wouldn't want anyone to think you read or anything like that."

"More like I had only just set up my shop and it was an open secret how much your entire family hated me for the simple fact of my existence. I recognized her from your store."

Right. We weren't exactly nice to him when he first came to town, afraid he planned on putting Mom's café out of business.

He sighed, eyeing Max again. "For once, he came through town, and we were going to catch up over a pizza. Like a couple of normal people."

"I'm sorry. If I had known we'd end up ruining your night, I would've had our meeting someplace else."

To say he looked skeptical would've been an understatement. "Would you really?"

I tried to keep a straight face but failed. "No way. I've been craving Angelo's for ages, and this was the perfect excuse to come over."

"I thought so." At least he grinned before stepping up to order a Margherita pie for him and Max. I crept over to the table in hopes of overhearing the conversation taking place without getting in the way of any flirting. Becca was clearly smitten. I only hoped Max was more interested in her than in the attention.

"So we've been thinking, you know, about ways to bring more people into the store. With tourist season wrapping up like it has, we've been brainstorming."

Max looked over his shoulder, out the window. "It looks pretty busy in town, even after Labor Day."

"We still have visitors over weekends throughout September, while the weather's warm. But if you came back in another week or two, you'd notice the difference for sure." Becca turned my way. "Right?"

I decided against acting surprised she would even acknowledge me. "That's true. And a handful of businesses on the boardwalk have already shuttered for the season. That will happen through the rest of the month, until only those of us who live here are left."

"I've always wanted to live near the beach. Being able to walk the sand every day and be so close to the ocean. There's nothing in the world that inspires me more than salt air." Max turned his smile on me, and I could sort of see why Ethan was so exasperated by him. It felt like every other thing out of his mouth was a line from a book he was working on, or something he hoped would show up in an interview somewhere.

I was spending too much time around Ethan, becoming a jaded grump like him. "I do like walking on the beach in the morning. It's a nice way to start the day."

"And then you end up finding things like diary pages in a bottle." Becca jerked a thumb in my direction. "If you want inspiration for your next book, Max, just spend a few minutes around this girl. She has a way of attracting mysteries."

"Is your new book a mystery?" I regretted the question the instant both of them looked at me like I'd grown a second head all of a sudden.

"True crime." His voice took on a gentle tone, the sort of voice I used when I was talking to my baby brother, or to Emma's dog.

"That's sort of his claim to fame." Becca was all smiles, but under the table? The little stinker kicked me.

I kicked her back while slapping my forehead for Max's benefit. "Of course. Sorry. You work around books all day and genres start blending together."

"Of course. I'm one author out of thousands. I have no illusions." Max shrugged, while Becca darn near fell off her chair in a swoon. What a shame that I left my smelling salts at home.

He narrowed his eyes at me, then snapped his fingers. "Of course! Ethan's mentioned you. The woman who owns the bookstore and keeps getting herself into trouble. Didn't he almost get killed over something to do with you?"

My mouth fell open and I searched in vain for something to say.

Ethan cleared his throat behind me. He'd finished ordering and now looked none too thrilled with his cousin as he plopped into a chair. "Very nice. No wonder you're a big-shot author, the way you use your words."

"I'm sorry. Really." Max looked sincere, at least. "I'm too blunt when it comes to things like that. Probably because I write about them all the time."

"Blunt, huh? It runs in the family." I gave Ethan a fake smile which earned me an eye roll.

"Are you in town to research your new book?" Becca obviously wanted to turn the conversation back to him. I found myself wondering if I should leave them alone.

"Yes and no. There's an auction taking place next week and I'm interested in one of the items up for bidding. I've had an interest in the woman whose things are being auctioned off, sort of puttering around with the idea of writing about her untimely demise." He moved his eyebrows up and down. "I drove out to the house earlier today and talk about inspiration."

Becca rested her chin on her palm, utterly entranced. "Who is it?"

"Una Howell."

"Oh, sure." I nodded slowly. "She passed away a few years ago, didn't she? I remember hearing about it. She lived in one of those big houses at the end of the cape." Not far from Driftwood, the Cornell estate. I shuddered inside at the memory.

"Right. And she died there." Again with the eyebrows. "There've been rumors ever since over whether her death was an accident."

Ethan made a slashing motion with both arms. "No. We're not getting into that right now. Some of us don't need an excuse to get involved with yet another mystery."

I mimicked him with my arms. "I'm going to pretend you're not talking about me."

Becca found a way to pump the brakes before we got into a fight—though her solution left me gasping, just the same. "Hey! If you're coming back to town for the auction, do you think you could maybe come in for a brief signing?"

I kicked her. I didn't bother trying to be gentle. "We can't put him on the spot that way."

"It's okay." Max's smile turned flirtatious. "Here I was, wondering how I was going to come up with an excuse to see you again. A signing would be the perfect opportunity."

Embarrassment threatened to kill me on the spot. I managed to overcome it long enough to choke out a few words. "You'd be okay with that?"

"Sure thing." He lowered his brow, though. "If you are. I'm sure that sort of thing doesn't plan itself."

Becca was almost bouncing up and down in her chair, buzzing with excitement. "I can handle all of that." Yes, and she most certainly would. This was her baby, and I wasn't keen on upending my life to accommodate her crush. No matter how valuable she was as an employee and friend.

"Then I guess we're decided." Max grinned at Ethan. "Where's our pizza? Did you order?"

Just when I thought I'd seen the entire range of Ethan's irritated expressions, he invented a new one on the spot. Somehow, it was different when somebody other than me was the one irritating him.

Probably because I sort of understood where he was coming from.

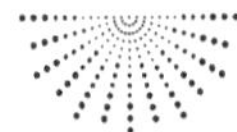

CHAPTER TWO

"Anyway, he's going to be at the store next Friday, the day after the auction. Becca's already hard at work, getting the word out about it. I made sure we'll be fully stocked with Max's books by then, but that's as much as I'm doing for this."

Mom wore a Mom Look when she turned away from the oven after sliding a muffin tin inside. "It's not like you to take such a negative view of something that could bring a lot of business to the store."

"I can't imagine how many people Becca will be able to bring in, considering the short notice. That's one thing." When Mom kept staring at me, I shrugged. "Well? Is that not enough?"

"You don't like her taking the reins. It's all right. You can admit it."

"It's not the fact that she took the reins. I wouldn't have had the nerve to come out and ask him to have a signing. But it's still my store. Right? Shouldn't we talk about things like that before we go ahead and put the idea out there?"

"Sometimes, you have to strike while the iron is hot."

"And sometimes, you shouldn't put people on the spot."

"Hey. That rhymed." When I didn't smile, Mom waved a hand. "You're overreacting."

"And you would know nothing about that."

"Watch it, young lady. You might be a grown-up with a business of your own and everything, but I think you forget who you're talking to."

"Sorry, sorry." I wasn't really sorry, and I wasn't really sure why the situation at Angelo's was still stuck in my craw the following morning. I settled for making patterns with my finger in powdered sugar left behind after sifting it over a tray of lemon bars.

Mom tossed me a rag to clean up the sugar. "I understand where you're coming from. You know how long it took me to bring in help around here."

"And yet I'm still doing grunt work for free at the crack of dawn. How does that work, exactly?"

"Boy, you woke up on the wrong side of the bed this morning."

This time I was genuinely sorry. "You're right. I need to get over it. And Becca apologized a million times after we left the restaurant. She clearly has a huge crush on Max."

"I'm sure she spoke before she thought about it. If you put a little effort into your dating life, you might know that."

If I wasn't careful, I would end up biting my tongue clean off. Mom had no idea about Ethan asking me out, nor did she have an inkling about him kissing me a while back. For one thing, I had never been the type to pour my heart out to her. She didn't need to know the ugly personal details of my romantic life.

The fact that it was Ethan added a whole other level of *no, thank you* to the situation. There'd been many things I was sure would kill the woman, but this seemed like it would do the job handily. While her loathing of Ethan had mellowed into mild dislike now that she didn't see him as a threat anymore, that didn't mean she'd push me out the door into his waiting arms, either.

"Whatever you do, don't let this writer pull you into another mystery. Please. Take pity on your poor mother." She patted my shoulder on the way past, rushing around the kitchen the way I'd watched her do for decades.

"I have no intention of getting into another mystery, believe me." I hadn't told her—or anybody—but there hadn't been a night since my showdown with Bobbi Cornell when she hadn't shown up in my dreams. The outcome was always the same, with Bobbi hurting Georgie before I could stop her.

That hadn't been the real outcome, thank goodness. Georgie was his usual happy, babbling self. He wouldn't remember that night or the way his big sister had wrestled a gun away from a maniac while he was only one room away, crying in his playpen.

"It wouldn't do your father any good, either." It was rare for Mom to bring him up so casually.

"You don't have to tell me that. I'm always worried about his heart."

"I'm more worried about him having a stroke when his blood pressure shoots through the roof. But I guess Holly does what she can to keep his temper in check."

Interesting. She said it so casually, the way she would if we were talking about anybody other than her ex-husband and his fiancée.

"Yeah, I'm sure she has her hands full." I glanced Mom's way from under my eyelashes, wondering where this would go.

Aside from Emma and me telling Mom about the engagement—which was roughly as fun and easy as sweeping for landmines—we hadn't talked about the upcoming wedding or the fact that Dad had decided to make it official after years of him and Holly living together. I wasn't going to change the subject if she wanted to discuss it, but I didn't want to lead her in any one direction, either.

She didn't keep me hanging long. "I think it's a good thing, the two of them getting married."

I did what I could not to fall off my stool. "You do?"

"Don't you?"

"He isn't my ex-husband, Mom."

"Don't pretend you were any more of a fan of their relationship than I was."

"I was wrong then." And when I thought of the time I wasted being angry and hurt and childish, I was ashamed of myself.

"I'm sure it has to do with him getting older, wanting to make sure Holly and Georgie are taken care of when he's gone."

I didn't love thinking about that. "And maybe Holly wants to be married. Maybe she wants a wedding, and he wants to give that to her."

"That's what Bob said." Ah, so she'd been talking it over with her boyfriend. His presence in her life was nothing less than a miracle for so many reasons. I knew there had to be plenty of things she didn't feel comfortable bringing up with me or my sister. She needed a partner, somebody to lean on.

I didn't even want to think about how tough the wedding announcement would've been to hear if she was still single.

"Bob's a pretty smart guy." I went to her and kissed her cheek. "I mean, he's with you, right?"

"Kissing up, huh?" She couldn't hide a little smile, though. "That's right. Keep kissing up. I'm still miffed at you for not telling me about that Cornell business."

"You were sick in bed."

"Not an excuse, young lady."

I checked the time and whistled. "Wow, is it that late already? I'd better get out of here."

"Sure. Run away." But she was chuckling as I ducked out through the back door, so I took that as a win. She'd get over the Cornell situation soon. What concerned me more was the wedding.

I wasn't the only one with concerns. My sister answered on the first ring. "What's wrong? Who needs what?"

I paused in the middle of stepping into the bookstore through the back door. "Huh?"

"You don't usually call this early in the morning, so I assumed it was an emergency." She paused. "Is it?"

"No."

"Oh. Good. So what's up?"

The woman was exhausting. I loved her, but dang. "I just left Mom's, and we were talking about the wedding."

"How did she sound?"

"Better than we expected. She's taking a very reasonable approach."

"That doesn't sound like Mom."

I laughed, flipping on the lights and taking a look around the store. As always, the sight filled me with pride. "I know. Bob's been a good influence."

"We owe that man something."

"No kidding. But what gift says 'thanks for keeping my mother sane and, as a result, keeping us sane as well'?"

"Not exactly the sort of thing you can say with flowers, is it?"

"No. Gift card?"

"Sure, a steak dinner will definitely balance out the scales." Emma moaned. "Steak. Mmm."

"It's barely seven o'clock in the morning."

"And? Ever hear of steak and eggs? Besides, it's for the baby."

"Man. That baby is quite a gourmet. Didn't you say they wanted a bowl of shrimp scampi yesterday?"

"And a side of roasted brussels sprouts and some chocolate cake. What about it?"

Right, and she wasn't allowed to eat sugar for the rest of her pregnancy. Joe probably needed a gift card, come to think of it. Did the liquor store carry gift cards? "Angelo asked about you when I was in there last night."

"Why do you have to rub it in? Do you know the cravings I've had for his pizza? Did you tell him I sometimes cry myself to sleep because I miss smelling his sauce through the floor?"

"You live three blocks away now."

"Which is three blocks further away than I used to. Jeez."

"Do you think you could make it all the way over here next Friday for a book signing? I know it's so far away now."

"Book signing? Who with?"

I told her about Max and Ethan and Becca's hopeless crush. "I can't wait for her to get in so I can torment her all day. She was practically one of those heart-eye emojis the whole time."

"He must be pretty cute."

"He looks a lot like Ethan, actually."

"Oh? And what does that mean, Darcy Harmon?"

I stuck my tongue out at the phone. "It means he looks like Ethan. Since you know what Ethan looks like, you generally know what his cousin looks like, too."

"You are so pitiful."

"Me?"

"You. Pretending you don't notice him. You think you're fooling anybody?"

My heart sank in time with me sinking into the chair in my office. "Who told you?"

Silence. Too much silence. "Who told me what?"

"Nothing. Not a single thing." *Shoot, shoot, shoot!* "I was kidding."

"Who told me what, Darcy? I swear, I will come down there right now. You will witness a pregnant lady throwing a row of shelves through the front window if I don't get a straight answer out of you."

I eyed my front window, visible from the chair. It looked a lot better in one piece. While I doubted Emma would throw an entire row of shelves... I would put nothing past freakish pregnancy hormones. Especially knowing how irritable she was without her beloved sugar.

So much for keeping the whole Ethan thing a secret.

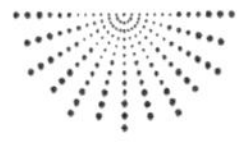

CHAPTER THREE

"Becca, I swear, you're going to worry yourself into an early grave at this rate." I finally had to step in after witnessing her bouncing around the store for three hours straight. With my hands on her shoulders, I held her still. "Take a breath. Relax. The signing is going to be a huge success, thanks to you."

At first, it looked like she wanted to argue with me. Her mouth screwed up like she was going to tell me I was wrong about things being great.

Then her shoulders slumped. "I want everything to be perfect. For us, of course."

Sure, this had nothing to do with Max at all. But I'd already teased her enough about him over the last few days. We were now two days out from the signing and I had to admit she'd done a fantastic job of getting the word out. There were announcements in the *Phil-adelphia Inquirer*, for heaven's sake, not to mention the papers in Paradise City and even down in Wilmington. "Everything's going to be perfect. We've gotten, what, twenty or thirty calls this morning alone." As if on cue, the phone rang. I rushed over to answer it, leaving Becca to continue fluttering around the store, arranging and rearranging the display we wouldn't use for another two days.

I had more than enough experience with frantic worrywarts. If I could talk my mother down from the ledge, I could certainly handle my frazzled assistant.

"There's a great write-up about the signing in the paper this morning."

I sighed at the sound of my sister's voice on the other end of the line. "No offense, really, but if you're bored enough to call over here once or twice a day, why don't you come over and handle the register for me?"

"Ew." Emma made a noise that sounded suspiciously like something Mom would do. It took pretty much all the willpower I possessed not to make the comparison.

"Well? I can tell you're bored out of your mind."

"It's not my fault the doctor doesn't want me traveling for work right now." Emma's career as a food writer usually had her bouncing from one place to another on a fairly regular basis. The baby had forced her to slow things down and work from home as much as possible, though her editor wasn't exactly keen on a bunch of articles about restaurants within driving distance. Normally, she'd be in Miami or Austin or LA.

"I'm just saying, either come down so we can talk face-to-face or save all your phone calls for one longer phone call at the end of the day. Jot down everything you want to say and we'll cover it all once I'm closed up and back at home. Easy peasy."

"You're a lot of fun, you know."

"So I've been told." The light for the other extension started blinking. "I have to go, there's a call on the other line. It's madness over here." She barely had time to say goodbye before I picked up the other call. "First Edition, Darcy speaking."

"You know, I can almost see you sitting in your third-grade classroom, ready to thrust your hand into the air the second the teacher asks a question. So eager."

"Ethan, it's very busy over here." Still, I had to smile, if only because he was absolutely right about me. If we'd been face-to-face it might've been a different story. "What do you need, besides a nicer personality?"

"I need a favor."

"You certainly led off like a man who needs a favor."

"I'm a notorious charmer."

"So what is it, then?" I looked over my shoulder to find Becca stacking hardcovers of Max's book. Nobody had ever stacked the same pile of books so many times.

"I need you to go to this auction tomorrow. With me."

"Huh? What auction?"

"The one Max was talking about last week."

"Sorry. I wasn't paying the strictest attention to that." Another glance at Becca before I lowered my voice. "I bet if you asked my assistant, she could recite the entire conversation verbatim."

He snickered. "Anyway, it's this auction going on at that dead lady's house. The one he was talking about."

"I remember that part."

"He was supposed to go and bid on this desk he's obsessed with, but now he's got some other thing going on. His sister planned something with their parents since he let it slip he'd be nearby, and he doesn't feel like he can get out of it without starting the next world war."

"I can't possibly identify with that."

Another snicker. "No, your family is notoriously even-tempered and reasonable. I told him I'd go for him and make the bid. So what do you say? Will you come with me?"

"Maybe I chose the wrong time of day to switch to decaf, but I'm still not following."

"I don't want to go alone. Probably a bunch of people like my cousin there. All snooty and full of themselves, paying obscene amounts of money for somebody else's junk."

"It's really nice of you to do this for your cousin."

"I wanted to get him off my back. Believe me, this has nothing to do with family loyalty or anything like that."

"Oh, good. I wouldn't want you to turn over a new leaf and become a nice person."

"Please? I'm asking as a friend. Will you go with me? I hate doing things like this alone."

Was this vulnerability? Maybe he'd turned over a new leaf, after all. Ethan wasn't the sort of guy who laid it on the line and admitted he needed help. Especially with something like this, something simple and low-stakes. "So long as we're not there all day. I don't know if you heard about it, but we're hosting a big signing on Friday and things are sort of wild around here."

"It'll only be a couple of hours. Bidding starts at nine, and the desk is the sixth item up for auction. Max already filled me in."

"Okay. Honestly, I wouldn't mind the excuse to get out of here for a little bit. Becca is… intense." I watched out of the corner of my eye as she positioned and repositioned a sign she'd rush ordered, featuring a photo of the book and copy from a few glowing reviews. She'd move it an inch or two, step back and consider it, then move it again.

"Thanks. I owe you one."

Yes, you owe me dinner. I resisted the impulse to blurt out that little gem. It had been more than a week since he'd asked me out and there hadn't been a word about it since. I told myself—not for the first time—to stop being so anxious and desperate to control every-thing. "Can I ask you something?"

"Depends on what it is."

"How many of your friends did you ask to do this with you before you called me?"

"The answer to that question is obvious. I don't have any other friends." But he was laughing when the call ended, so even if that was true, he didn't mind.

Was I his only friend? I didn't know whether to feel bad for him or not.

"What do you think?" Becca tapped my shoulder and gestured toward the display.

"I think it looks fantastic." And it did. I wasn't just saying that for her sake. "Listen, do you think you could handle things around here for a few hours tomorrow? Ethan begged me to go to that auction Max was talking about. Max can't make it, so Ethan's going to bid on the desk for him."

I hadn't expected her face to fall. "Max can't make it? Is he sick? Oh, my God, if I went to all this trouble—"

"No, no, he's fine. A family thing. No big deal." I took a deep breath and motioned for her to do the same. She followed suit, then we exhaled together. "Keep doing that, okay? Everything's going to be perfect. And I'm sure Max will have nothing but gratitude for all the hard work you've put in."

She exhaled, but I wasn't sure she believed me.

I winked. "Maybe he'll come up with an interesting way to express all that gratitude."

"Quit it." She scowled at me before responding to a customer with a question. It was nice to see she still possessed the bandwidth to care about them or anything, really, beyond her massive crush.

Max's book sat on the front counter, where I'd been paging through it whenever I had a few minutes free. He was a compelling writer, no doubt. I could see why he made the list, why there were book clubs out there choosing this particular true-crime story as their pick of the month.

"It's great, isn't it?" Becca noticed me reading as she passed the counter.

"It's a real page-turner. I don't read a lot of true crime, but this is super compelling."

"You don't? Oh, I do. I love it. I have, like, half a dozen podcasts I listen to religiously."

"About murders?" I couldn't help wrinkling my nose a little. "That's creepy."

"Spoken like somebody who never listened to one. Come on, don't tell me you've never watched one of those investigative reporting shows."

"Yeah, who hasn't?"

"It's the same thing. And sometimes these writers and podcasters end up uncovering new clues the authorities never touched. Like the Golden State Killer. Tons of regular, everyday people researched like they were getting paid to do it, and they ended up helping find the guy."

I set the book aside, looking at my friend through new eyes. "Wow. You possess hidden depths."

"You should see the subreddits where I hang out. All kinds of ghoulish, real-life murder stuff there." There was a touch of glee in her voice when she said it. I couldn't relate to her interest, but I knew I had no room to talk, either. I had a habit of getting involved with murders and other unpleasant situations. When I looked at it that way, Becca's hobby was downright normal. Safe.

It was a shame Halloween was still six weeks away. We'd certainly be setting the spooky stage with a bunch of true crime aficionados hanging around.

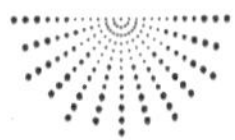

CHAPTER FOUR

"It's great that you didn't bother to dress up for this. Casual is the way to go." I looked Ethan up and down with a thumbs up when we met in front of the Howell mansion.

He looked down at his usual work outfit: black t-shirt, jeans, sneakers. "I have to get back to the store after this. What, was I supposed to wear a suit?"

"I'm kidding. Lighten up." I elbowed him on the way into the building, where signs were set up to direct visitors on where to go. Good thing, since the place was absolutely enormous.

"I almost wish I knew more about how Una died. Didn't Max say she died here?" I looked up at Ethan, but he was too busy scowling and surveying the people and things around us to notice. "Becca's a true crime buff. She would've been the better choice to come here today. At least she could soak in the atmosphere."

That, he heard, and he came to a stop in the middle of an ornate entry hall. "You talk like you're not into it."

"What?"

"You heard me. You're talking like unsolved crimes and mysteries and all that don't make your pulse race."

"They don't."

"Untrue. You don't even hear yourself, do you?" He clasped his hands together over his chest and raised his voice in pitch. "I wish I knew more about how Una died." He even fluttered his eyelashes for effect.

"I didn't sound like that."

"You sounded like a breathless fan. Trust me, I've met enough of them while spending time with Max."

"I thought you were going to say you hear it enough when people rave about your amazing food."

He snapped his fingers. "I'm slipping. That's what I should've said."

"Anyway, you're wrong. Crime isn't a hobby for me." It wasn't until I said it that I realized just how loudly I'd said it, and how many people were around us at the time. A couple of them gave us wider berth, glancing at me as they did it.

Ethan noticed, too, and clearly loved it. "Whatever you say."

I wanted to smack the smirk off his face.

Instead, I deliberately turned my attention to the house. Like Driftwood, it sprawled out in all directions, and the many windows on the southern-facing side afforded a breathtaking view of the ocean. Unlike the Cornell mansion, Una Howell's hadn't been renovated and modernized. The heavy drapes, thick carpeting and ornate... everything... made me think Una's mother had decorated the house and nobody had touched it since.

Ethan studied a pair of lamps up for bid. "Would you ever buy something like this?" He leaned in to inspect the bases, shaped like a pair of mermaids and painted gold. The shades were seafoam green glass with clear shell-shaped beads hanging from them.

I cringed. "No, not my style." I couldn't imagine them being anybody's style, but who was I to criticize? Ethan, on the other hand, looked like he could hardly rein in his criticism. No big surprise there. "But somebody else might like them, so shush."

"Okay, okay. Guess all the money in the world can't buy taste." A man standing near us heard him and looked our way.

I mouthed a pitiful apology while taking Ethan by

the arm and yanking him away. "Would you stop with the commentary? You're going to get us kicked out, and then what would Max say?"

"Fine, fine." We entered a big room where chairs were set up in rows and heavier pieces of furniture were lined up along the walls. People strolled around, taking notes, eyeing each other in passing. Like predators at the watering hole, wondering who they'd have to fight for their next meal. My imagination was running wild, in other words.

"Wait. There are two desks." Ethan came to an abrupt stop. "He didn't say there'd be another desk."

"Maybe he didn't know." I looked back and forth from one desk to the other. Both were clearly well-made, worlds away from the particle board desk in my apartment. Something told me neither of them needed to be assembled after purchase.

"Which one does he want?" He pulled out his phone and snapped pictures of both desks, then sent them to Max. "Honestly, I'd love to know how he plans on getting either of them home."

Good point. They both looked like they'd take at least three people to move. "I never thought of that, either. He could hire a crew to drive it, I guess?"

"Not my problem, either way." He checked his watch. "They'll be starting soon. He needs to get back to me if he expects to win this thing. I could be working right now."

"Relax, would you? Take a breath." It was a good thing he'd asked me to come with him. I didn't want to imagine how many fights might break out if he was left to his own devices. "Do you have a limit you're allowed to bid?"

"He said up to five thousand dollars."

It came out before I could stop myself. "Are you kidding?" I clamped a hand over my mouth, horrified, as the chatter around us ceased. I might've shouted it.

Ethan snorted out his laughter. "And I'm the one you're worried about?"

"But that's a lot of money for a desk. What's so special about it?" I couldn't see anything about either of them that, to my mind, warranted that sort of price tag. "Did he tell you anything?"

"Do you think I listened?"

I narrowed my eyes.

He relented. "He might have. But seriously, I was half-listening. I do remember him saying something about the guy who made it and what a big deal he was. That's probably why."

"At least that makes sense." Yet when I thought about everything I could do with five thousand dollars, it still didn't seem like a worthwhile buy.

"What do I know? I threw out all my dolls and stuff when I turned ten. I'm sure I could earn a fortune selling them online today."

"Let me guess. They were all in perfect condition, just like the day they came out of their boxes."

"There's nothing wrong with being conscientious." Good thing his phone buzzed when it did, before he had the chance to say something sarcastic.

"It's that one." He pointed to the simpler of the two pieces. "And now he says I can go up to seventy-five hundred if need be."

My eyes bulged at the thought. There had to be something special about it. Leave it to Ethan to tune his cousin out when he was saying something important.

We weren't the only people interested in the desk, either. The man who gave Ethan a look when he criticized the lamps was hanging around nearby. He'd wander off to look at something else but always came back, eyes darting around like he couldn't help but size up the competition. He looked to be somewhere in his forties, with a slight paunch and a stooped posture. Wire-rimmed glasses kept sliding down the bridge of his nose—he adjusted them in time to shoot a furtive look my way.

I elbowed Ethan, then nodded as discreetly as I

could in the man's direction. Ethan's jaw tightened before he let out a soft grunt like he understood. The sight of his narrowed eyes left me hoping he wouldn't take a swing at the guy. After all, he was already in a mood over having to be there.

"Behave yourself." I tugged his sleeve to make sure he was listening.

"Are you kidding? This finally stopped feeling like a waste of time." He even cracked his knuckles, for heaven's sake. Ready to go to war over a desk. All things considered, it was better than pouting.

"Ladies and gentlemen, the auction is about to begin." A man in a suit stood at the front of the room, smiling wide. "Thank you for your interest. If we could fill these chairs, please." He swept an arm over the area in question, and in no time people started filling in the rows. We snagged two seats near the back while the man in the glasses sat near the front. I couldn't help watching him.

The first item went up for bidding at exactly nine o'clock, a beautiful old settee covered in rose-colored silk. The next was a pair of armchairs. According to the man leading the event, all three pieces dated back to the early twentieth century.

Ethan leaned over to murmur in my ear. "It's amazing. They look brand-new."

"Maybe they were covered in plastic all these years?" He covered a laugh with a cough as bidding continued. There were around fifty of us in all, and five bidders volleyed back and forth, topping each other with each new bid. It was like watching a tennis match, my head snapping back and forth every time somebody called out a new number.

I had to catch my breath after the chairs were declared sold. "This is actually kind of exciting, isn't it?"

The man looked like he pitied me. "You need more excitement in your life."

"So I've been told." That didn't make me change my mind, though.

Finally, the fifth item came up for bid. It was our turn—no, Ethan's, not mine. I was only there for moral support. I reminded myself of this as the auctioneer introduced the desk and offered a little bit of history. I finally realized we could've picked up all this information if we'd grabbed brochures on arrival, but we'd been too busy sniping at each other.

"We'll start the bidding at five hundred dollars." Okay, this could end up being more reasonable than I'd imagined.

Ethan raised his hand. "Five hundred."

I made a mental note to tease him later over the way his voice got deeper when he called it out.

"Seven-fifty." That came from the guy in front. Another bid, this one for a thousand dollars. I started sweating like it was my money involved.

Ethan raised his hand. "Eleven hundred."

"Twelve-fifty." The guy in front, who glanced back at us over his shoulder. There was no mistaking his irritation. Meanwhile, somebody else bid thirteen hundred. "Thirteen-fifty."

Ethan growled loud enough for the people in front of us to shoot him a look. "Fifteen hundred."

"Two thousand." Now glasses guy looked straight at Ethan.

"Twenty-two hundred." Ethan held his gaze from across the room.

"Twenty-five hundred."

"Three thousand." That was almost a shout.

I squeezed his arm as tight as I dared but he ignored me in favor of shooting a death glare at his new enemy. The rest of the room had gone quiet, with all the other bidders giving up in favor of watching the drama unfold.

Ethan's opponent adjusted his glasses. "Thirty-two hundred."

"Thirty-three."

"Thirty-five."

"Thirty-six." Their voices almost overlapped, they bid so quickly. I looked down at Ethan's hands, clenched into fists so tight the veins in his forearms stood out.

There was a moment of silence, hesitation on the part of the other guy. Ethan snickered softly before muttering under his breath. "That's right. Give it up, pal."

He didn't. "Thirty-seven hundred dollars." A few people grunted their approval while others shook their heads in amused disbelief.

Ethan's jaw twitched. "Four thousand."

"You realize you don't have to jump a few hundred dollars at a time, right?" Though I whispered it, a handful of people around us heard me and laughed.

Mr. Glasses was starting to sweat. He looked at the desk, then at Ethan. "Forty-one hundred."

"Forty-two." By now, this felt like the most important thing that had ever happened. Nothing in the history of time had featured stakes nearly this high. I held my breath, waiting to see if there'd be another bid.

Mr. Glasses wanted to. His mouth was in a line so tight I couldn't see his lips anymore. His face had started to go from red to nearly purple. "Forty-three." He didn't sound so sure of himself anymore.

And Ethan heard it. "Forty-four." There was satisfaction in his voice, not to mention the way he sat back in his chair and folded his arms.

I murmured out of the corner of my mouth. "You don't have to gloat." He only snorted, eyes still on whom he now clearly saw as the enemy. An enemy he'd all but decimated.

The auctioneer looked from one of them to the other, waiting for more. "That's forty-four hundred dollars going once... forty-four hundred going twice..."

"Forty-five hundred." Mr. Glasses wiped sweat from his forehead, glancing over his shoulder to where Ethan was now ready to boil over.

The words tumbled out of my mouth before I could help it. "Forty-six hundred!" I bit my lip, mortified, while the people around us snickered and chuckled.

Ethan did neither of those things. "What are you doing?"

"I got caught up in the moment." And now I had to hope Glasses would counterbid since I certainly didn't have that kind of money for a desk.

The auctioneer let out a surprised little laugh.

"Forty-six hundred." He looked down at Glasses, his brows lifting in silent challenge.

"Forty-six-fifty."

Ethan truly didn't want to give up. I almost felt sorry for him. Every bid came slower, his voice a little quieter. Like he didn't want to step aside but knew he was in over his head.

"Forty-seven." Ethan shook his head a little, muttering under his breath. "Give it up, man."

"Forty-seven going once..." The auctioneer looked at Glasses, who shrank in his chair. "Going twice... Sold for forty-seven hundred dollars." There was light applause at the announcement, while I fell back in my chair with a sigh of relief. My heart was still racing, and over something that didn't affect my life one way or the other.

Ethan was the picture of self-satisfaction when he stood. "Come on. I have to arrange delivery before getting back to work." He turned away from the front of the room and didn't see Mr. Glasses shooting him an absolutely filthy look.

But I noticed. And I felt sorry for him.

Though, to be honest, I was also sort of proud.

CHAPTER FIVE

"It was way more exciting than I would've guessed." I finished putting away the last of my laundry, then took a look in the closet for ideas on what to wear for the signing. It seemed like an event requiring a little more than my usual everyday clothes, but I didn't want to get too dressed-up, either.

In other words, I was in the middle of a very exciting Thursday night.

Emma giggled in my ear. "I bet it was exciting."

"What's that mean?"

"It means you've been practically breathless the entire time you described what happened this morning." She giggled again. "You'd think the guy struck oil or cured cancer, when all he did was win at an auction."

"It was exciting."

"I'm sure it was."

"You had to be there."

"I'm sure that's true." She was still laughing at me. "But don't even pretend Ethan didn't play a big part in the excitement. If it was anybody else bidding, you wouldn't have gotten half so wrapped-up in it."

"That's not true at all."

"Mm-hmm."

I dropped onto my bed with a groan. "I should never have told you about us."

"Oh, there's an us now? Is there something you're not telling me?"

I hated when she got like this. Smug, teasing, unwilling to let it go. "No. You know what I'm getting at. I wish I hadn't let it slip."

"I'm sorry. But how often do I get the chance to tease you about anything?"

"I don't keep a running list, but you do it a lot."

"No, I don't, because you always have things together."

That made me laugh. "Please."

"It's true! You've always been the level-headed one. The dependable one. The successful businesswoman."

"You haven't done so badly yourself."

She made a dismissive sort of snorting noise. "Apples and oranges. Not the same at all. And don't even act like you haven't felt at least slightly superior more than once."

"Nope. Not ever." I wished we were Facetiming so she could see the look on my face. "Ew! Did you really think that?"

"Um… yes."

"Um, you're wrong. If anything, I've been jealous of you sometimes." It wasn't easy to admit, but it was true. "You were always traveling. Having adventures. Meeting people, seeing places. Meanwhile my life never changed from one day to the next."

"Oh. I never thought of it that way. All I saw was you giving me a hard time about getting in trouble and taking risks and whatever."

"Okay. Maybe I took just the slightest bit of pleasure in that after feeling jealous."

"Mm-hmm."

"Anyway, I don't have all my stuff together. Sorry to disappoint you. And I'd love it if you wouldn't get on my case about Ethan. Seriously."

"Since when do we not tease each other? Want me to list all the things you've teased me over in the past few days alone?"

"No, thanks." I had to laugh, since she had a point.

"Anyway, he's a sore spot. Things are weird. Let's leave him off the table, okay? As a personal favor."

"Why is it weird?"

"Because he told me he wants to go out but never said anything else. Is this some kind of test? Or a game?" I got up and went to the kitchen to boil water for tea. I needed something to help me unwind before going to sleep, and I was still too keyed-up from the excitement of the auction and Becca's wild, almost frantic energy as she put the finishing touches on the signing arrangements.

"This is going to sound wild, but hear me out. Why don't you talk to him about it?"

I cringed at the very thought. "You are a sick, sick woman."

"And you're chicken."

"Am not."

"No? So it's not chicken to be too scared to ask a guy why he won't take the next step and actually discuss dinner plans? Come on."

I set the kettle on the stove with a sigh. "It's not that easy. He's prickly and tough to understand. I don't want him thinking I'm making a bigger deal out of this than I need to."

"It seems pretty easy to me. Ask him what his deal is." She paused. "Or I can, if you want."

"Don't make me kill you."

"You wouldn't kill your pregnant sister."

"Try me and find out." I eyed the knife block on the counter. "And I'd wait until the baby's born, obviously. I'm not a total monster."

"I shudder to think of what my mother-in-law would do to my child if I wasn't there to stop her."

"That is a very good point."

She groaned. Loudly. Dramatically. "Fine. I'll be a good girl tomorrow and not say anything to him when I come in to work the register for you, since I'm such an incredible and generous sister."

"Please. Like Ethan would show up." I pulled a box of tea from the cabinet, a blend that was supposed to be good for sleep. "He can't stand being around Max when he's around his fans. I think you'll understand why when you meet Max tomorrow. Mr. Personality, all the way."

"It's exhausting to be around somebody like that. I guess for somebody like Ethan, it would be even more uncomfortable."

"He doesn't suffer fools or flatterers."

"Which is probably why he likes you, because you're neither of those things."

My mouth fell open. "I never thought about it that way."

"You would have if you had opened up to your sister before now. Just think about all the pearls of wisdom you've missed out on."

"Okay, okay, let's not blow things out of proportion." I fixed my tea, reflecting on what she said. It made sense. He appreciated the way I didn't bother flattering him. I didn't hesitate to call him out when he was acting like a jerk, either.

Leave it to Emma to throw me a curveball. "Have you talked to Pete lately?"

"Wow. You're pulling out all the stops tonight, aren't you? Really making sure I feel good and miserable about my personal life."

"I'll take that as a no, then."

Pete Frazer and I had a complicated history, to put it mildly. "I'm sure he's still counting his blessings after being rid of me." Though I still sometimes caught a faint whiff of olive oil in the kitchen, reminding me of the mess we both ended up sliding around in before I almost kissed him. Before he informed me he was seeing somebody else.

"He's single again. I can't help but think he dumped that girl because of you."

"Or because she was leaving town soon and he figured he might as well get it over with. I'm not going to go down that road again. It's too messy." Not to mention embarrassing. The memory of that night on the kitchen floor was enough to make me cringe in horror almost two weeks later.

It was always like that. I could barely remember what I had for dinner last night, but bring up an embarrassing moment and it was like I was right back there, going through it again.

"Anyway, I hope all the trouble we went to was worth it. Max had better keep that desk around for the rest of his life and hand it down to his children." I fixed my tea, remembering how determined the man in the glasses was to be the winner. I had told Emma about him and, of course, she'd gotten a kick out of my description of things. But she hadn't seen the crushed-yet-furious look on the guy's face.

"I wonder what was so special about it."

"You can ask Max tomorrow, if you want."

"Thanks for granting permission, Mommy."

I chose to ignore that little dig. "Maybe Max is writing a book about her. How she died, all that. Though I can't imagine there being much worth writing about—not enough for an entire book."

"You never know. Some people can spin up a story out of almost nothing."

"I'm sure you're not speaking from experience."

"Oh, shush—" Joe cut her off, speaking in the background. I couldn't make out what he was saying but heard the tension in his voice.

"What's wrong?" I stopped halfway through making my tea, listening hard.

It took a second for her to answer. "Apparently there was a break-in. It was just called in at the station and apparently, somebody had to tell my husband about it because he's not allowed to have a night off."

I decided against telling her how much she sounded like our mother, who used to complain about the exact same situation when she and Dad were together. It became an almost nonstop refrain after a while, to the point where I wondered how much of Dad's constant work had to do with avoiding their crumbling relationship.

Instead, I asked the most logical question, the first that came to mind. "Where was the break-in?" I checked the time and found it was barely past ten. Late enough for somebody to think they'd get away with it.

Emma's hesitation made the hair on the back of my neck stand at attention. "Em? Where was it?"

"He's fine. Keep that in mind, okay?"

My chest tightened. "Where was the break-in?"

"At Ethan's. Somebody broke in. But he's fine."

I decided to find out for myself.

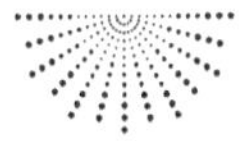

CHAPTER SIX

"I'm fine." Ethan spread his arms before turning in a slow circle. "See? Not a scratch on me. I might've missed the whole thing if he wasn't so loud about it."

For the first time since I heard about the break-in, I was able to take a deep breath. The pounding in my chest started to slow. "You're sure you're okay?"

"I'm telling you, I barely even caught sight of the guy before he was out the door. If I was injured, it'd be because of my own clumsiness, trust me." He tipped his head to the side, eyes narrowing into slits. "Why are you here, anyway?"

That was a good question. There were officers milling around, dusting for prints and taking photos of the scene, but then they had an obvious reason to be there. I, on the other hand, did not. And now that I knew for sure there was nothing wrong with Ethan beyond what had always been wrong with him, I felt sort of silly for having literally run there.

Yes. I ran. Though I still didn't have a working car after crashing it thanks to Greg Cornell cutting the brake lines, and I had been in a hurry. What else was I supposed to do?

Still, my explanation felt flimsy. "I was on the phone with my sister when Joe got word of your call. I freaked out, I guess."

"Hmm." He folded his arms, frowning.

Which had the effect of setting off firecrackers in my head. "Why the attitude? I'm sure you're not used to people caring, but surprise, it's possible."

"I wouldn't have expected it. That's all." He relaxed his posture. "Thank you. Seriously. It means a lot, knowing you care."

I took a peek inside the house through the front window. The living room was visible, brightly lit thanks to every lamp being turned on so the cops could do their job, and the sight of the desk Ethan had only just won made me gasp in dismay. "The desk! It's ruined!"

He grunted. "Yeah, it looks that way, doesn't it?"

Somebody had taken a screwdriver to it. And a hammer. There were bits chipped off. Deep gauges in the wood. One of the drawers had been pulled out of its track and smashed on the floor, where it had splintered all over the place.

"Why, though?" I couldn't take my eyes off it. All that money, and now the desk was ruined. "Why would anybody do this?"

"That's what we're trying to find out."

My head snapped around at the sound of Pete's voice. He was coming out of the house, walking slowly while scribbling something down in a notepad. Darn it, we were just talking about him, weren't we? And darn him for looking as cute as ever, though it shouldn't have come as any sort of surprise. It wasn't like years had passed since the last time I saw him.

He looked up at me, his mouth a thin line. A beat later, he nodded. "Good evening. What brings you here?"

So that was how he wanted to do this? Pretend like we were nothing but passing acquaintances? Fine with me. "I was on the phone with Emma when Joe got word about this. I thought I'd come by and make sure..." Why did I feel guilty? I had nothing to feel guilty over.

Something passed over Pete's face. Sort of a grimace, but then it didn't last long so I wasn't quite sure what I was seeing.

Whatever it was, it inspired me to keep babbling. "I was at the auction this morning, where Ethan won that desk for his cousin. I can't believe somebody would ruin it like that. And after all the money it cost, too. Max never even got the chance to use it." I looked at Ethan, who rubbed the bridge of his nose between his thumb and forefinger.

"He's going to have a fit. I don't blame him. He spent the better part of five grand on the desk—"

Pete grimaced for real this time. "That was a five-thousand-dollar desk?"

"Close to it." Ethan looked through the window at what remained. "What a waste."

"What's so special about this desk?"

"Beats me. You would have to ask my cousin about that." Ethan turned to him. "I was bidding on it in his place. He's due to reach town early tomorrow morning."

I piped up, trying to be helpful. "He's doing a book signing at my store."

Pete shot me a look that snapped my mouth shut. "If you wouldn't mind, I'd like to speak to one of you at a time." Ouch. He was in full cop mode at this point. I might as well have been a stranger. Even if he didn't mean to come off quite so snappy, I couldn't help but feel deflated.

Ethan brought to mind a bull getting ready to charge when he lowered his brow. "As I was saying, he's due in the morning. He was going to arrange for a moving company to get the desk home. I should never have let them bring it over here. I told him I'd rather leave it at the mansion and let him take care of it, but he insisted."

Pete tapped his pen against the notepad. "Did he say why he was so insistent on getting it out of there?"

Ethan shrugged. "He's been nothing but sketchy about this whole thing. He wouldn't tell me why the desk was worth so much or why he was so protective of it."

Meanwhile, I was practically bursting out of my skin, desperate to get a word in edgewise. Why was Max so protective of the desk? Why was it worth so much? Why would someone break into Ethan's home, vandalize a stupid desk, then take off?

"What about your things? Was there anything out of place that you could see? Did the burglar take any of your valuables?"

The three of us looked through the window. I had never seen the inside of Ethan's house before and was refreshingly surprised by how nice it looked. Not fancy or expensive, but coordinated. Like he'd put actual thought into the furniture and whether he'd be comfortable. What had I expected? Dorm room chic? The desk was sitting in the middle of the room, like he'd left it where the delivery company had placed it.

He shrugged. "It doesn't look like they touched anything else."

Pete nodded as he checked his notes. "We're picking up a lot of prints, but nothing much on the insides of the drawers that were pulled out and broken —we figured that would be where the burglar would've left them, versus the people working the auction and what have you. It seems like they were fixated on the desk, whoever they were. Did you get a good look at them?"

"Nothing I would give to a sketch artist if that's what you're asking. I didn't really see his—her?—face, and the light in the living room was off when I came downstairs. I had just finished showering, and when I turned off the water, that's when I heard the noises coming from down here."

I shivered, imagining what that had to be like. Granted, he was a man and might've been able to protect himself better than I would have in that situation, but still. For a person to think they were alone and safe—not to mention how vulnerable people were when they were bathing. There was a reason that shower scene in *Psycho* still resonated after sixty years.

"What did you do then?"

"I put on a towel and went downstairs."

Yes, Pete had put me in my place for butting in, but I couldn't help it. I gasped, one hand over my mouth. "You just went right downstairs? What if they had a gun?"

"They didn't, did they?"

"But what if they did? Did you even think about that?"

"Sorry if I wasn't doing much thinking. I was reacting. And don't act like you've never waltzed straight into trouble without thinking twice."

"Okay, okay. You're getting off track here." Though judging by the way Pete's mouth twitched at the corners, I had a feeling he agreed with Ethan. I wanted to bang their heads together. More than once.

Ethan grunted. "Anyway, whoever it was had already started for the door. I barely wrapped my head around what I was looking at—the mess on the floor, I mean—before I finally noticed them making an escape through the front door."

"Man, woman?"

"A man. Average height, average build. Nothing out of the ordinary about him, aside from the fact that he had no business being in my house."

"I need you to close your eyes and really concentrate. What was he wearing?"

From the way he snorted, I could tell Ethan wasn't a fan of this, but he went along with it and closed his eyes anyway. "Dark pants. A gray shirt, long-sleeved. A black ball cap with the brim pulled low. But he never turned around. I didn't so much as catch his profile."

"Could it have been a woman in men's clothing?"

Ethan's thick brows drew together, but he shook his head after a few moments. "No. It was definitely a man. I can't tell you exactly how I know. I just do."

I had a feeling that wouldn't be enough for Pete, and I wasn't wrong. "The way he moved?"

"That, and the general build. Boxy. Slim hipped. You know what I mean."

"Sure." Meanwhile, I found myself wondering if men got together behind women's backs and compared their bodies for fun. There was almost a sort of shorthand passing between the two men in front of me. They weren't friends that I was aware of, but they seemed to understand what the other was saying.

I was on the verge of asking whether they wanted to be alone for this when Ethan snapped his fingers. "He had something under his arm! I can't believe I almost forgot about it."

"What was it?" I couldn't help myself. I could feel Pete scowling at me but ignored him in favor of grabbing Ethan by the arm.

"A book. He had a book." He looked at Pete. "I'm sure of it."

"Did you happen to get a look at it?"

"Just enough to see that it was a book. Hardcover. He sort of jammed under his arm like a football and ran out with it." He even went so far as to demonstrate.

"Do you think the book came from the desk?" Yes, that made the most sense, but both Ethan and I shook our heads.

"No, the drawers were empty. I checked them myself once the desk was delivered, and I didn't put anything in it." Ethan ran a hand over the back of his neck, sighing. "I never thought a simple piece of furniture would end up giving me a headache like this."

Meanwhile, I was practically jumping up and down, bursting with what seemed obvious to me. "What about the other guy?"

"What other guy?" Pete had the nerve to sound annoyed when all I was trying to do was help.

"At the auction. There was another guy who really wanted that desk. They had a little bidding war."

"I had forgotten about him." Ethan chewed his lip,

his forehead wrinkling like he was concentrating hard. He shook his head. "No, I don't think it was him. This man was smaller. The one we saw today was more on the husky side."

"Please, one at a time." Pete went so far as to adjust his body, sort of wedging himself between me and Ethan with his back facing me. "Can you describe the man from the auction?" Ethan did so without my input, since I was afraid to breathe too loudly, much less say anything. So this was how it was going to be? I thought Pete and I had moved past this point.

"Thank you for all your help. If I need anything else, I'll give you a call." The two of them shook hands before Pete turned his attention to me. I almost wished he wouldn't since he was being so rude. "Now, as for you."

"I think I'm going to go inside." Ethan rolled his eyes behind Pete's back. "Thanks for coming by, Darcy. I'll stop in at the store tomorrow during the signing." I bit my tongue rather than beg him to stay with me, since I very much had the same feeling I used to have on the rare occasions I'd be called to the principal's office.

"Exactly why did you come over again?" Pete's pen was poised over the notepad.

I glanced at it. "Is that an official question, or a personal one?"

Just when I thought his frown couldn't deepen any further. "This isn't a game."

"I'm aware of that, which is why I came as fast as I did. I heard a friend of mine had a break-in, and I wanted to be here for him." I cocked my head to one side, hands on my hips. "It's called being friends. Remember that?"

"Okay, okay. Fair enough." His posture relaxed a little, until he was almost a man I recognized. "This is a pretty strange situation all the way around."

"Well, if I were you—"

"Which you are not."

"—I would talk to Max Greene when he's in town tomorrow. There has to be something about the desk he didn't tell us. Why else would it be important enough to risk breaking into somebody's house?"

"What if the burglar only vandalized it because that's as far as they got before Ethan found them? There doesn't necessarily have to be anything deeper going on. And trust me, whoever it was, they did their best. There's wood everywhere." He looked through the window again, grimacing at the mess.

It was like talking to a wall. I wanted to shake him but settled for tapping his arm to pull his attention back to me. "I'm telling you, it was the other guy from the auction. He really, really wanted it. Maybe he decided if he couldn't have it, nobody could."

He didn't try hard to hold back his distaste. "No offense, but that sounds like something from the plot of a romance novel gone wrong."

I winced, though it wasn't like this was the first time I'd ever heard such a thing—and the derision behind it. "Do me a favor and spend less time with my father. You sound way too much like him right now."

It was his turn to wince. "Point taken." He looked back at his notes. "But then there was the book. Where does the book come in? And why am I even discussing this with you?"

Dang it. I was sort of hoping he would continue verbalizing his stream of consciousness, if only because I was insanely curious and had at least a tangential connection to the situation. "I'm telling you. I bet it was the other guy who wanted the desk. He was so determined, and crushed that he didn't win the auction."

"Thank you very much, Detective." Pete slid the notepad into his pocket, followed by the pen. "Now if you wouldn't mind, we have to wrap this up. If there's anything else I need to know—"

"You'll call me. I know. I've been through this before."

"Yeah. No kidding." At least he grinned, and it was a genuine one that took years off his face. Now he looked more like the Pete I knew and liked best. "And good luck with the signing tomorrow. I passed by yesterday and saw the poster in the front window. Sounds exciting."

"Between you and me, I could use a little less excitement in my life." I could've asked why he merely passed by rather than stopping in, but something told me we would only end up arguing if I did. Besides, he had work to do, and I was now more in need of a cup of tea to calm myself down than ever.

Though something told me it wouldn't work.

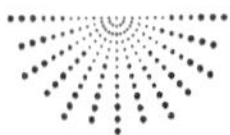

CHAPTER SEVEN

I had never seen my sister as excited as she was the morning of the signing. Well, maybe one other time, when she happened to be at the supermarket when the bakery employees were about to throw out a few sheet cakes which they gave her to take home, instead. That was a joyous day she still sometimes talked about in a hushed, reverent tone of voice normally reserved for religious experiences.

With that in mind, the morning of the signing came in second place. I knew the rosiness in her cheeks had nothing to do with Max or the number of people already hanging around outside the store, waiting for him to arrive. It wasn't pregnancy glow, either.

"I hope he'll be able to put on a happy face after

knowing he wasted five thousand dollars." She was doing everything but giggling in glee as we waited for Max to arrive. The woman was dying to see how he took the break-in. Had pregnancy made her morbid and nosy—or was that genetics?

"Forty-seven hundred, and he better be able to." I glanced over at Becca, who once again rearranged the stack of books on both ends of the table where Max would sit in all his glory. "Otherwise, this was all for nothing. I hope I didn't invite all these people out here just so they could be disappointed in their favorite author."

I lowered my voice to a whisper. "And it would crush her."

"I know. She's the one I'm more concerned with." Emma called out to Becca, giving her a thumbs up. "It looks amazing. You're a superwoman, I swear."

"I don't much feel like it." Becca twirled a strand of auburn hair around her finger, glancing toward the window while biting her lip. She wore a dress I had never seen before—which made sense, since she never wore a dress around the store. "We're supposed to start in fifteen minutes. Where is he? I was hoping there'd be time for him to read a little bit from his book but now I don't know."

"I sent him a text. He said he's on his way." Though

half an hour and passed since then, and I hadn't heard anything else. Ethan had most likely gotten in touch with him about the desk by now. I hoped the bad news hadn't made him forget his commitment.

A few minutes later, the three of us heaved a sigh of relief when a car pulled up in front of the store. Becca ran out and moved the folding chairs she'd put up as a last-ditch effort to make sure there was a spot for Max to park. Meanwhile, the crowd outside buzzed with fresh excitement, whipping out their phones and poising them to snap a shot of their hero.

Their hero who did not look very pleased. I braced myself for what was coming while he quickly crossed the sidewalk and ducked into the store. He was wearing an almost painfully hip outfit, his chunky cardigan covering a T-shirt with a deep V cut that showed off a hint of his chest. I was pretty sure a couple of the girls outside swooned.

I did not swoon, but I did wear my biggest smile. "Max. It's good to see you."

"It hasn't exactly been a red-letter day. First, I get the news about the desk, then traffic is a nightmare." He ran a hand through his hair, making it flop forward onto his forehead. "I need coffee. I didn't have time to stop for coffee."

Emma and I exchanged a look that told me we

were on the same page. Becca, meanwhile, was only too happy to be helpful. "I can run next door and get you a cup. Did you eat? Are you hungry?"

At least he grinned, even if it was a brief one. "No, thanks. Just coffee, black. Thank you." He sounded warmer, too, which I could tell came as a relief to her.

Once she was out of the store, I showed him to the table. "Becca has worked extremely hard to get this set up in such a short amount of time."

He nodded his approval. "I have to admit, I didn't expect to see so many people out there."

"She took this very seriously."

He shook out his hands, then rolled his head back and forth. "I need to shake this off. I'm sorry, but hearing about the desk this morning really threw my entire morning off. I'm sure you've heard about it by now. There can't be that many break-ins in a town like this."

"You might be surprised." Emma joined us, arms folded, and there was no mistaking the hard look she gave him. "Our father was a detective, and my husband is one, too. We get our fair share down here."

"If I didn't know any better, I would think you were bragging about the crime rate."

I understood where Emma was coming from,

though. Max made it sound like we were some useless little town.

He flashed his broadest, most dazzling smile. "It was a compliment, trust me."

Emma was unmoved.

"At least Ethan wasn't hurt." I was trying to be helpful, trying to remind him of what mattered—to my mind, anyway.

"Of course, of course." Yet he still wouldn't loosen his jaw, and his scowl remained firmly in place. It had to be genetic, that scowl. He looked more like Ethan than ever when he wore it.

Becca hurried in with steaming coffee. "Folks are getting restless outside. There are even people waiting next door, in the café." I was surprised she didn't curtsy after handing the cup to Max, who accepted it with a soft grunt before downing half the cup at once.

Meanwhile, Emma was still staring at Max in a way that made me wonder whether having her come in as back-up was such a hot idea. "You'd better hustle over to the counter." I went so far as to take her by the wrist and pull her away from Max, who was oblivious to the death stare he was receiving.

"What a creep." My sister curled her lip in a sneer.

"Calm the hormones, please. Let's make nice. There

are a lot of people coming in here—and if this is a success, we might be able to make this a regular thing."

"Not with him, I hope." She jerked her chin in Max's direction. Good thing Becca held his attention. I couldn't hear what they were talking about but she was taking notes, so I imagined it had something to do with any last-minute rules he wanted to put in place.

The phone rang and Emma answered, then put a hand over the receiver. "It's Mom. She says open the doors already so these true-crime nuts will leave her café, because they're starting to upset the regulars."

"Oh, for heaven's sake." I took the receiver from her. "Since when do you mind a little crime talk in the café? You practically live for it."

Mom replied in a fierce whisper. "Gossiping is one thing, but describing a murder scene in stomach-churning detail is another. It's making me nauseous."

Yikes. "We're just about ready to go here, anyway, so I'll open the door. But not because you told me to." I handed the receiver over and waved a hand to catch Max's attention. "I'm going to open the door now and have everybody follow the arrows to form a line."

Becca had even gone to the trouble of making tape arrows on the floor, directing fans through the store.

Please, please let this go well. I took a deep breath before unlocking the door again and opening it wide.

"Come on in! Welcome. Please follow the arrows on the floor. Thank you for coming out. Welcome to *First Edition.*"

Most of the crowd was female. That much jumped out at me immediately. Several of them not only carried copies of Max's most recent book, the one we'd made sure to stock up for anyone who wanted to buy a copy at the signing, but they also held his previous works. I hoped they didn't expect him to sign all of the books, since the authors at every signing I'd ever been to had a rule against that. They couldn't afford to sit all day, inking up book after book.

And something told me Max wasn't in the mood this morning.

Though he at least looked friendly enough, warm and cordial as he greeted the women at the front of the line. "This is a real treat. I don't often get the chance to chat with my readers." He flashed one of those million-dollar smiles and I was pretty sure I heard a few hearts shatter.

Becca cleared her throat, stepping up in front of the table. I had to bite back a smile at the way she held herself, so regal and imposing. She was the chick in charge of all this, and woe to anybody who thought otherwise. "One book per reader, please. You'll be invited to provide your name, but any further personalization won't be possible. Photos are allowed, and you are invited to step behind the table to include Mr. Greene in the picture, but we request that be held to one photo per customer." Meanwhile, there were still people waiting outside now that the store was full, so they didn't hear any of that.

Emma was reading my mind. "I'm sure Becca won't have any problem repeating herself when the time comes."

All of a sudden, a hurricane dressed in a leopard-print caftan and matching ballet flats burst into the store. "I know I'm late, I'm sorry." Trixie kissed both of our cheeks before elbowing her way back to where Max was sitting. She thrust out a hand while raising her sunglasses with the other. "I'm a reporter for the *Cape Hope Times*. Just call me Trixie."

"It's very nice to meet you." Max looked roughly as overwhelmed as most people generally were the first time they met Mom's best friend.

"Excuse me, excuse me!"

I should've known Aunt Nell would be right behind Trixie, since the two of them were practically inseparable. Along with Mom, they enjoyed activities such as putting their noses into our business and asking awkward questions at inappropriate times. Nell had run the town's library for as long as I could remember, so it made sense she would be eager to meet a bestselling author.

Still, there was some grumbling in the ranks as ladies who'd waited all morning were none too thrilled with what looked like Nell cutting in line. And these weren't local ladies, either. They didn't know who she was, and they didn't much care. I plastered on my widest smile while ushering her back to the front counter.

Her cheeks flushed as pink as her cardigan. "I just wanted to say hello. Why did Trixie get to go say hello?"

"Because Trixie is writing about this for the paper, and you know that." At that very moment, my auntie was muttering something into her phone, which I knew meant she was recording notes for her piece. "You can say hi later. But please, let's not start a rumble here in the store."

Nell grumbled, but in a good-natured way. "What's the use of having an inside connection if I can't take advantage of it?"

"Don't get your hopes up too high." Emma was still far from impressed, giving Max stink eye from across the store. "He's prickly. And I'm being nice when I say that."

"I have an idea. Let's keep our opinions to

ourselves until later. Much later." I shot my sister a look that left no room for interpretation.

She rolled her eyes but shrugged. "Fine. We can talk later about what a pain—"

"Hi!" I stepped aside, ushering a customer closer to the counter. "Emma will ring up your book. I'm so glad you could come out and see us."

Nell, meanwhile, did her best not to laugh. She was just as bad as Mom, if not worse. Always stirring the pot, then standing back in pretend surprise.

After an hour, even my sister couldn't complain about Max's way with the customers. He was charming, self-deprecating, cracking jokes with the fans and even providing little bits of behind-the-scenes info on his research and other topics when they came up. He went so far as to smoothly recommend other related books stocked nearby, too. "If you liked this, you'll love that series. Becca has it right over there. I'm telling you, I couldn't put it down once I started."

Becca was all too happy to point people in the right direction, naturally.

This was a good idea, after all. We'd started out a little bumpy but everything had smoothed out. The register never stayed closed for long, and everybody seemed happy both when they were coming in and while they were leaving.

It was perfect.

Until Ethan pushed his way through the crowd still waiting to get in. His face was red, his eyes practically shooting fire. His head swung back and forth until he found Max—and his hands tightened into fists.

Not a good sign.

I intercepted him before he could storm through the store. "What are you doing? The signing is still going on in case you couldn't tell."

"What am I doing?" While I'd whispered, he couldn't be bothered to lower his voice. "I'm here to kill him, that's what." The store went quiet, all eyes on us now.

Becca went pale, dismayed, while Trixie's eyes danced with merry light. She always did love a little drama.

The only person who didn't look surprised was Max. "I wondered how long it would take you to get here."

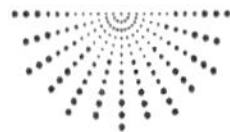

CHAPTER EIGHT

"So that was fun." I leaned against the counter, elbows propped on it, then dropped my head into my waiting hands. "Next time, let's set the store on fire and challenge everybody to get out before the smoke gets too thick."

"It wasn't that bad." Emma rubbed my back in slow circles. "Everybody was happy when they left, and Max managed to keep things moving smoothly. Only Becca seemed ready to murder Ethan."

"She'd have to wait her turn."

Ethan was in my office, where I'd ordered him to go after making a scene. The last arrival had just left with a tote bag full of new books. We had a lot of restocking ahead of us.

First, to find out what the heck was going on. "You

can come out now." The office door opened and Ethan emerged, looking slightly less fiery but no less angry. A half-hour alone hadn't done much to settle him down.

"What the heck is going on?" I looked at Max, then at Ethan.

"You haven't figured it out yet? I thought you would have by now." Ethan's flared nostrils and twitchy jaw didn't give me much confidence. I was roughly three seconds from ordering both men outside—but then, let's be honest, I wouldn't have been able to listen in. Not to mention my sister and aunts, all three of whom were doing everything but eating popcorn, waiting for the fur to start flying.

"Figured what out?"

Ethan growled. "You want to tell her, or should I?"

"What am I missing?" When Ethan nodded to Max, I stomped my foot. "No. You. Out with it. What am I missing?"

He glanced around and I finally understood why he was hesitant. I met Emma's gaze. Her shoulders slumped. "Come on, ladies. Let's go next door so I can torture myself, looking at all the goodies I can't eat until the baby comes." The furtive glance she shot me as they left spoke volumes. I'd have to fill her in once the dust settled. Of course, I expected nothing less.

Once it was the four of us, with Becca looking concerned if not completely aware of what was going on, I turned to Ethan again. "Now. What did you come barging in here and make a scene over?"

Ethan pointed to Max. "He didn't tell me why the desk was such a big deal. You should've come clean with me. Anybody with half a brain could tell there was more to that desk than you were letting on."

He jerked his thumb at me. "Even she knew there had to be something bigger going on."

My head snapped back. "Uh, thanks. Glad you think I have half a brain."

"You know what I mean." Ethan scowled at me. "And if you weren't distracted by the signing and Mr. Wonderful over here, you would've figured it out by now. Why would somebody go to all the trouble of breaking the desk up when none of the drawers had locks on them? Why did the burglar have a book under his arm when he left my house?"

Becca smacked her forehead. "Of course, you had a burglary. You okay?"

"I'm fine." He mustered a small smile. "Thank you. Strangely enough, the burglar only cared about the obscenely expensive desk my cousin begged me to bid on. The desk he was willing to spend seventy-five hundred bucks on if it came to that."

I thought back to the mess in Ethan's living room, the splintered wood all over the floor. The gouges in the desk. Somebody had gone to a lot of trouble to… do what?

"Because you cared more about that desk than you did about your own cousin, things could've gone badly last night. What if whoever broke in decided to shoot me? Or fight or something else? What if I had a gun in the house and shot him? It would've been your fault."

Max smirked. "Technically no, since it wouldn't be like I sent them to you."

That was a mistake. At least keeping Ethan off him kept me from taking a swing, myself. "Calm down." I put my hands on Ethan's chest and tried to ignore the thumping of his heart under my palm.

Finally, it hit me. I whirled on Max. "There was a hidden drawer in the desk, wasn't there? And you knew about it, but you didn't want anybody else to know."

"It's about time." Ethan threw his hands into the air. "Yes. A hidden drawer. There was too much wood left over for it to have all come from the visible drawers, so it finally occurred to me to get on my hands and knees and look around underneath. That's when I found the mechanism used to release the hidden drawer back before the hidden drawer got smashed."

Max's face worked like he was trying to come up with something to say but falling flat.

"Well? Why didn't you come clean with Ethan?" And me, but that was secondary. He had no way of knowing I'd go to the auction—and this had nothing to do with me, anyway. I had to remind myself of that, no matter how I wanted to jump in and fight for Ethan's sake.

Where the heck was that impulse coming from? The man could take care of himself.

Max blew out a long breath. "You're right. I should've told you why the desk mattered so much. I never imagined it would make a difference, though. That's the thing."

Ethan snorted. "Aren't writers supposed to have great imaginations?"

"You know what I'm saying." Max glanced at Becca, but she didn't look as sympathetic as she might have earlier. He knew he was outnumbered, and the knowing showed itself in the downward turn of his mouth. "Yes. I knew there was a strong chance of the desk containing a hidden drawer."

"How did you know that?"

"Victor Reynolds, the man who built it, was known for including hidden storage in his pieces. Dressers, desks, even bookcases. He was big deal back in the early twentieth century. I was researching Una Howell, wondering if there was enough there for a book, and I found pictures of the home's interior in an old architectural magazine. The desk was in one of the pictures, and Reynolds's name was mentioned."

"I still don't understand why that means anything." I looked from Becca to Ethan and found them both as confused as me.

Max ran a hand through his hair, lifting a shoulder. Almost sullen. "It has to do with Una. Now that I'm explaining it, the whole thing sounds ridiculous. At least, I know it would to you."

"You don't know me at all, so how would you know what I think is ridiculous?"

"I know he will." He jerked his chin at Ethan, who responded with a blithe shrug that said more than any words could. "Right."

"So, the dead lady owned a desk with a hidden drawer." I held up one finger, soon followed by a second. "The hidden drawer got busted up last night at Ethan's. He saw—"

"—a book under the burglar's arm. A book that came from that drawer." Ethan raised an eyebrow. "What was in the book? Why was it so important?"

"If it's what I think it is, it's something people have been looking for and speculating on ever since Una died. Her last diary, the one she was writing in at the time of her death."

Dang it. Dang it so hard.

Somehow, intrigue was starting to sneak in, pushing out my righteous anger. I practically tingled at the idea of a lost diary and what it might hold. Was I as hopeless as Ethan accused me of being?

Ethan was not as impressed. "How do you even know she was writing one?"

It was Becca who spoke up. "She was well-known for her diaries. She kept them her entire life." When I raised my brow in surprise, she shrugged. "Like I told you, I'm into a lot of true-crime stuff. And since she was from the area…"

Max took it from there. "Her diaries are like a time capsule. Anybody who ever stayed with her—and a lot of people did, she did a lot of entertaining back in the day—saw her writing in a diary at least once while they were at the house. She wrote in them every night before going to bed."

"So she died and her last diary was missing." Ethan was the only unimpressed member of our little group, but then that hardly came as a surprise. It took a lot to impress him. "And you guessed it must've been in the desk drawer."

"Exactly. The fact that her diary was never found is

one more reason for the people interested in the case to suspect she was murdered."

"Murdered?" Ethan blurted out a laugh. "That's kind of a leap, isn't it?"

"Not when you know the facts." Max folded his arms and for all the world could've been Ethan's twin when he scowled. "She fell down the stairs one night and broke her neck."

"Wow. That never happens." Ethan rolled his eyes.

"The autopsy revealed a sedative in her system."

"Again, completely unusual. Nobody ever takes sleeping pills."

"Only she didn't." Becca slid a guilty look Max's way, like she worried she was speaking out of turn, but he nodded. "She had an aunt who overdosed on sleeping pills. Probably an accident—she'd been taking them for years and years and developed a tolerance. Una avoided them because of that. She didn't drink, either."

"Exactly. Her doctor swore he never wrote her a script, too. And there was no record of her getting any from the pharmacy she always used. Her housekeeper was the only member of the staff who lived on the premises, and she was visiting family out of town at the time, so somebody else must've been with Una at some point the night she died." Max lifted a shoulder.

"I mean, what does that tell you? Doesn't it seem suspicious?"

"Sure. I can admit that much." Ethan held up a hand before any of us could react. "But! This is all pretty thin. A lot of supposition holding everything together."

"Yet here we are, after somebody broke into the desk and took a book from it. A book you weren't aware was inside." Max's grin was evidence of his knowing he had proven his case.

Though that didn't help him as far as I was concerned. "So what you're saying is, you knew all this. You suspected a hidden diary that might point to her killer. Yet you never thought to clue your cousin in on this before he had the desk brought to his house."

"Right!" Ethan was mad all over again. "You wouldn't even let me leave it at the mansion. No wonder. You were afraid somebody would break into it. Well, surprise, they did, only it's my locks that now need to be replaced."

Max scoffed. "You know I'll pay for that."

"You'd better pay for that."

I stepped between them again before Ethan could lunge. "Okay, okay, let's all take a breath before we do anything we'll regret."

"Don't assume I'll regret it." Ethan's smile was chilling, directed straight at his cousin.

My head spun after learning all of this. A possible murder, and now the possible evidence had been stolen from Ethan's. By… whom?

I looked his way. "You're sure it wasn't the guy from the auction?"

"What guy from the auction?"

I glanced Max's way. "The guy who ran the bidding up as high as it went. He was set on that desk, but he didn't have the money to keep bidding."

But Ethan was adamant. "Like I told Pete Frazer, I don't think it was him. Totally different builds."

"What if he paid somebody to do it for him? Or a friend, somebody you wouldn't recognize? Maybe he figured you'd know him from the auction and didn't want to risk it."

"Hold on. What are you saying? You think the other interested bidder was the one who broke in?"

I should've tried harder to hide my disdain, but it had already been a long day and my patience was remarkably thin. "Yes, that's what I'm saying. Pretty plainly, in fact."

Becca's face fell but I didn't feel sorry. Max had already been way more trouble than he was worth, yet instead of being humble and admitting he'd messed up, he still had that arrogant tone in his voice.

"You realize it'll be impossible to find him, right?" Ethan sighed, an almost pained sound. "Why do I feel like that doesn't matter and I'm talking to myself?

I was already way ahead of him, planning to call the auction house in charge of yesterday's event. "Gee, I have no idea."

CHAPTER NINE

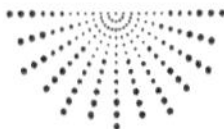

"I'm sorry, Miss. I'm not sure how we can help you."

I dug my nails into my palm, willing myself to sound cheerful. "There's no way you can help me identify someone from the auction yesterday?"

"I'm afraid not. There was no registration process. Unless somebody won an item up for auction, there is no record of their name or the fact that they were here at all."

It made sense, even if it didn't thrill me. Calling the auction house responsible for the event was the first effort, a dart throw while blindfolded. All I could do was hope the dart hit the board. I didn't expect a bull's-eye on the first try.

Though that didn't exactly make it easier to run up

against a brick wall. "Were there any pictures taken? Professionally, I mean?"

The woman on the other end of the phone snorted softly, like she wanted to laugh. "No, I'm afraid not."

I wanted more than anything to get off the phone, if only so I could stop feeling like a total idiot for even calling. Still, there was that stubborn part of me—the Harmon part of me—that wouldn't allow it.

"Here's the problem." I dropped the sunny, cheerful note from my voice, becoming more serious and professional. "I attended the auction, and a friend of mine won an item up for bid. The item was taken to his house, and within hours was vandalized. Now, it seems to me the only people who would be aware of the item's arrival would be other people who attended the event. Do you agree?"

Silence. I waited, tapping my fingers on the counter, while Becca watched from across the room. She was in the middle of restocking our mysteries and true crime thrillers. She raised an eyebrow, questioning silently, and I gave her head shake.

Finally, there was an answer. "Exactly what are you getting at?"

"What I'm getting at is, somehow, someone in attendance managed to find out where my friend lives. Either that, or they followed the delivery truck that dropped the item off at my friend's home." Time to fib a little. "Now, I've been working with the police department in Cape Hope, and from what they've deduced, the burglar focused solely on the Victor Reynolds desk. So either this was a case of someone following the truck, as I said, or there was some sort of data leak on your end. Which is it?"

"Obviously—"

"Obviously, it would be a lot easier if you could at least give me the names of the people who won items yesterday. That's all I'm asking for. There's no law against that, is there?" When she hesitated again, I decided to go for the kill shot. I could only hope she wouldn't call me on it. "Of course, I could contact detectives Harmon and Sullivan from the police department. Maybe you would give them what I'm looking for."

Becca cringed, but gave me two thumbs up just the same. I closed my eyes, also cringing at my audacity. I wouldn't have blamed the woman if she hung up on me.

"Where can I send the list?"

I pumped a fist in the air and Becca did a happy dance. I rattled off my email address and was told to keep an eye on my inbox, that the list of names would be there shortly. "But only names. No other identi-fying information."

"No problem. I really appreciate your help." My hand was shaking as I ended the call, and I slumped against the counter. "Gosh, I didn't like that at all."

"You sure sounded like you did." Becca lifted her chin, one hand on her hip. "I'm sure they would hate to have to go to the police with this. It was a good move."

"Yeah, and I hope Dad and Joe never find out I dropped their names so casually. It makes me feel icky."

"Well, if those names get us somewhere, it won't have been for nothing."

So it was *us*, was it? I smiled to myself and decided not to point out Becca's choice of words.

"You can tell that to Joe the next time he comes around looking for my head so he can put it on a spike." I opened my laptop and pulled up my email, and was surprised to find a new message waiting. "Wow, she was fast."

"Because you scared her, of course." Becca joined me, the two of us poring over the list. Naturally, none of the names jumped out at either of us. "Forty-five people? Geez, that's a lot of research."

"Are you chickening out?" I nudged her with my

elbow, grinning. "You were the one all gung-ho about getting to the bottom of this."

She blushed. The girl actually blushed. "Well, I sort of felt bad for Max when Ethan came in ranting and raving." My mouth fell open, but she held up a hand. "Please. I know what you're going to say, and you can save your breath."

Fat chance of that happening. "Come on. I know you like him, and this isn't really his fault, but the tension between him and Ethan goes a lot further than this situation. And it's not up to you to fix it."

"I just sort of feel bad for him, I can't help it." She shrugged before going back to stocking. "I mean, he spent a lot of money on that, and now it was for nothing."

"Hey, he still has a perfectly good desk. It's a little scarred up, but…"

"You know what I mean. He was hoping to use that diary."

"He was hoping to use that diary for his own financial gain. That's what he was hoping to use it for." I knew she was going to argue, but it was my turn to hold up a hand to stop her. "We both know that's why he wanted it. He wanted to write a book about Una Howell. Maybe he still can. Let's not look at him like he was doing it for anybody but himself, okay?

He's not a saint. He's a writer looking for his next project."

"Fair enough. But I still sort of want to be a part of this." She slipped the books into place with a lot more force than she needed to, making them bang against the backs of the shelves. She wasn't usually like this, and I felt bad for taking a dig at Max when I knew how much she liked him. But facts were facts. He wasn't a kind or benevolent person. He wasn't trying to get justice for Una, either.

Clearly, we would never see eye to eye on this, so I figured it was better to let the subject go. I turned my attention to looking up the names in the email, finding whether they had social media accounts and one by one eliminating the people I didn't recognize.

~

"Since when is anything easy?" Poppy poured herself another glass of wine before joining me on the sofa, where my laptop was open in front of me.

"I was sort of hoping the guy settled for the other desk, or for something else being auctioned off." None of the people who'd won items at the event were the man who'd fought so hard to win Max's desk.

"What I want to know is, did the guy know about the diary?"

"I've been wondering that myself. Why else would the desk be that important?" I groaned, rubbing my tired eyes. "I swear, that Max. The things I want to say to him."

"I can't blame him."

I turned to my friend, my mouth wide open. "You're kidding me."

She waved a hand, making a dismissive noise. "Please. He's an artist."

"What's that supposed to mean?"

"It means sometimes an artist has to go above and beyond to create their art. I don't think having his cousin bid on the desk is so far out of the ordinary."

"He should've told him why the desk mattered. If somebody did kill Una and their name is in that diary, and the diary was in the desk, it meant putting Ethan in the killer's crosshairs. Possibly."

"I don't disagree with you. But if I knew there was an item out there somewhere that might potentially hold the key to what could end up being a fantastic piece, something I can be really proud of, I wouldn't stop at anything to get my hands on it."

"Anything?" I dipped my chin, raising an eyebrow.

"Okay, obviously, I wouldn't kill anybody. I

wouldn't steal it, either. And Max didn't steal it. He paid a lot of money." She swirled the merlot, staring into its blood-red depths. "It was a gamble. It might have paid off if it wasn't for that burglar."

"Of course, this is all still theory. Even if it was the diary in that drawer, it doesn't necessarily hold the key to how Una died." Though the thought alone was enough to make my skin tingle. It was a hunch, a feeling.

"Of course. But come on, you read more than anybody I've ever known. Even if there weren't any clues in there, it could have provided insight into her mental state or whatever." Another hand wave. "It could make for some compelling reading. The way you described it, there are people practically salivating over her unsolved death."

"Oh, you have to see this." I pulled up another tab, one which Becca had opened earlier at the store. Things were still a little chilly between us by the time I locked up for the night, but she'd at least gotten over being annoyed with me long enough to point me in this direction. "There's an entire board devoted to mysterious deaths in this part of the country. Una's name comes up more than once in a few threads."

Poppy leaned in to read some of the messages, then

shuddered. "That's creepy. Dissecting a dead person's life like that."

"I feel the same way, but it's obviously an incredibly popular pastime."

"But then here you are, doing your own sleuthing. Where's the line, what's the difference?"

I opened my mouth. I closed my mouth. Did she have a point? "I'm interested in this because it means something to me."

"Why does it mean something to you?"

"Because my friend was burglarized. He could've been hurt."

"He wasn't hurt, though, was he? The only thing that burglar hurt was the desk."

"Hey. You know it's deeper than that. Having your home broken into, I mean. It sort of makes a person lose that feeling of security."

"You're very protective of Ethan, then, aren't you?"

"No! Not really." I giggled helplessly and wondered why I was giggling.

"Sure, whatever you say." She winked before picking up my empty glass, holding it up in silent question.

I didn't usually have more than one glass at a time, but this was a Friday night. Granted, I had to work in the morning, but two glasses didn't mean I was partying or anything. I nodded my acceptance and she got up to pour more for me while I mulled over her question.

Was she right? Was I no better than some of these people who pored over the facts and theories of a case, exchanging ideas, coming up with wild notions of whether a person's death was accidental or something more sinister? Even to me, my excuse fell flat. Just because I was vaguely associated with the situation didn't mean I had to jump in headfirst and start offering vague threats to perfect strangers over the phone.

Maybe Ethan was right about me. Maybe I did get a little more of a thrill from sleuthing, as Poppy called it, than I ever realized. I had never really thought about it before. Following my instincts and doing what felt right came as naturally to me as breathing. It hadn't even occurred to me to step aside and let Joe and Pete and everybody else handle this—then again, there wasn't really enough evidence of any sort to convince them to investigate, either. They had actual work to do. But I still wanted whoever did this to answer for it.

Did that mean I had to take everything on my shoulders, though? It was all too confusing, with too many layers and too many questions. And it was more than I wanted to think about after a very long, very busy day.

Which was why I closed my laptop and put it aside in favor of chatting with my friend.

Even if the stranger from the auction sat firmly in the back of my mind, waiting for me. Daring me to learn who he was and why the desk had meant so much to him.

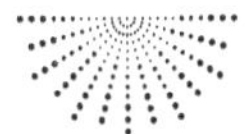

"Hi there, Pete." There was no reason for Becca to raise her voice like she did, not really. Not unless she wanted to warn me that Pete had entered the store, which was clearly what was on her mind when she called out to him.

I froze like a deer in headlights, my eyes darting around my office like there was anything around that could help me. I'd spent the past hour boxing up books, printing labels, processing orders. Before that, I had been in the basement, going through old boxes and doing some basic decluttering.

There was tape stuck to my shirt and maybe even in my hair. I ran a hand through it just in case and was horrified when dust came floating down and landed on my desk. Why didn't I have a mirror in my office? And maybe a makeup station and somebody to perform touchups when I needed them?

In other words, I felt like a troll who'd just crawled out from under a bridge. What a perfect time for Pete to show up.

"Hey. How's it going? Lots of excitement here yesterday." It seemed like Pete might've raised his voice a little, too, so I could hear him clearly. "I hope you did plenty of business."

"It was one of our best days in the past few quarters. Definitely something we should pursue in the future. I'm sure we'll get better and better every time." Becca was back to her normal, cheerful self, determined to turn *First Edition* into a massive success. Even in my panic I smiled to myself.

"Is your boss in?"

"She's back in her office, preparing orders. Maybe you can help her get them down to the post office?" Sneaky girl.

"You know me. Always eager to help." The sound of his approaching footsteps made my stomach flutter in a way I really wished it wouldn't. Things with Pete were too complicated. I couldn't afford to crush on him again, not after being humiliated when he was staying at the apartment. There were no hard feelings on either side—that much I knew—but still. I didn't want to go through that again.

I made a point to look busy, scarcely looking up from the box I was packing when he appeared in the doorway. "Hi there. What brings you in?"

"I wanted to have a chat with you."

I snapped my fingers. "Darn it. I was hoping you were going to say you want to volunteer your time. I have about a million orders to catch up on." The stack of boxes and envelopes already waiting on my desk testified to that.

He whistled, nodding slowly. "That's encouraging to see."

"Definitely. Now that things in town are so quiet again, we'll need all the help we can get."

"Is there anything I can do?" Oh, he was definitely there to either ask me something or tell me something he knew I wouldn't want to hear. Otherwise, he wouldn't be this helpful.

"Actually, I'm almost finished." I patted a stack of five books still waiting to be packaged. "Otherwise, I wouldn't mind a little help getting these down to the post office before it closes."

"Well, I swing past on my way to the station, so I'd be happy to lend a hand."

I finally looked straight at him, folding my hands in

my lap. "Okay. This was very nice, but you will come out with it now. What really brings you here?"

He grinned, maybe a little sheepish. "I spoke to Ethan. Actually, he came in and wanted to update me on what his cousin told him about the desk." Then he pointed at me, his grin widening. "And that is exactly what I expected you to do."

"What did I do?"

"Your face fell."

"It did?" I patted my cheeks. "I didn't notice."

"Why are you disappointed that he did the right thing and came to the police?"

"I'm not disappointed."

"You are so bad at lying."

"I'm not lying!" That was a lie.

And he knew it, judging by his wry chuckle. "What's it going to take for you to realize this is what I do for a living? That I'm the one who's supposed to be investigating things, not you?"

"Do you honestly mean to tell me you have the time and the bandwidth to handle something like this? It was a basic break-in. Nobody got hurt, there was hardly any property damage."

"Spoken like the daughter of a detective."

"Funny, since that's who I happen to be."

"Still." He was stern, his grin dissolving. "This is my

job. And even if manpower was stretched thin down at the station—which it isn't right now, since yours is not the only business that slows down once the tourists leave for the season—that's not your concern. That's up to us to manage. Not you. And I doubt this burglar poses a threat to anybody else in town."

"How do you know that?"

"Like you said. Basic break-in, minimal property damage. It was a targeted burglary, and we both know it. You have no reason to get involved." He sighed, falling back and leaning against the wall. "Though I know that's not going to stop you."

"I'm curious. The more I learn about everything involved, the more interesting it is."

"Then hang out on those message boards where people talk about true crime, then. Listen to podcasts —or create one of your own. If you're so interested in solving crimes, that's a perfect hobby for you." Then he laughed. "Now you wrinkled your nose. You have a very expressive face. Did you know that?"

"I do?" That time, I truly hadn't realized I was making a face. I wished he wasn't so observant, but then again that sort of came with the job. Or maybe the job came naturally as a result of his observational skills. A true chicken and egg situation.

Either way, I didn't much like the feeling of being

patted on the head and told to go play while the grown-ups handled the important things.

"Look." He glanced out toward the sales floor, then lowered his voice like he didn't want to be overheard. "I understand you better than you think I do. Don't argue with me. You're curious, you have a quick mind. You're also very smart."

"Thank you."

"When is enough going to be enough? Why can't you do what you like to do safely?"

"Behind a computer screen? Is that what you mean?"

"That is exactly what I mean. Because people who try to solve crimes from behind a computer screen are the ones who don't end up having to wrestle the gun away from a crazy lady."

His words had the effect of a bucket of ice water pouring over my head. I sat back in my chair, breathless now, my heart racing. Everything from that night came rushing back—it was never far from the forefront of my mind, anyway, though I did everything I could to block it out. My fear, my rage, my indignation at the thought of this woman having the audacity to break into my father's house and threaten not only me but my baby brother.

The next thing I knew, Pete was on one knee, beside me. "Breathe. Just breathe." It was not until then that I realized I'd started hyperventilating. He placed a firm hand against my back, between my shoulder blades, and pushed me forward. "Put your head between your knees. Just breathe." At some point, his other hand found mine, and he gave it a firm squeeze. "You're safe."

Yes. I was safe. It was behind me, weeks in the past. Georgie was fine, healthy and happy. Nobody hurt him, and no one had hurt me. My chest loosened, my heartbeat started to slow, and the roaring in my head quieted.

Once I could breathe, I sat up to find Pete still hovering.

His face was a mask of worry. "I'm sorry. I didn't mean to do that to you. I didn't realize—"

I shook my head, feeling sorry for him. He looked genuinely dismayed, his eyes pained as they moved over my face.

"It's okay. I didn't expect that to happen, either." I settled back in the chair, taking deep breaths. The world didn't feel like it was about to spin off its axis anymore. "I'm fine."

"You sure about that?"

"Positive. Don't worry, that doesn't happen all the time. In fact, that's the first time it's ever happened." When he only shifted from worry to skepticism, I groaned. "Sometimes I get a little panicky when I remember it, but I would think that's normal, right? I mean, if I acted like everything was fine and nothing happened, wouldn't that be a bigger problem?"

"I guess you have a point, but I don't have to be happy about it." He stood with a sigh. "But I hope you see what I mean. It doesn't have to be this way. Let us do our jobs, and you turn your considerable energy and intelligence toward making your business bigger and better than ever."

It was easy to nod. Easy to at least pretend we saw eye to eye. And I understood what he was saying, that I had to stop taking risks. That some of the things I did started out completely innocent and ended up getting me into trouble.

But darn it, I was still Sylvia Harmon's daughter. And with that came a heaping dose of stubbornness. I never did much like being told what to do.

"I doubt they'll go any further with the investigation."

I noticed Holly looking my way once Dad announced that. He had been at the station earlier in the day, checking in with everybody, sticking his nose in here and there. He couldn't let go, even with Joe having stepped up to fill the considerable void left behind once Dad made the decision to retire.

Obviously, Holly understood what he didn't, that admitting something like this was probably the last thing he should've done.

"Pete made it sound like they were pursuing it, though." I picked at my salad, bouncing Georgie on my knee. The kitchen of my father's house had long since been cleaned up, the sliding glass door replaced. Nobody would ever suspect what went on in this very room.

"Maybe they will, but I've seen too many things like this. There are no leads. There was hardly any damage done, and even Ethan didn't sound like he was desperate to find who did it. The crime had more to do with the desk than it did with him."

"You don't know that for sure, though."

Holly stepped in, smiling gently. "Is this more about the burglary, or about Ethan?" When I looked her way in surprise, she winked. The stinker.

"Please." I pretended to be more interested in

Georgie than in the question, but Holly wasn't about to be refused.

"It's okay to admit you're worried about your friend." She was trying very, very hard to pull something out of me. At least Dad was oblivious, too busy checking to make sure the steaks he'd just pulled off the grill had rested long enough. How he knew whether they rested long enough or not was a mystery. That was why he was the grill master and I wasn't.

"I'm not worried about him. At all. He's fine."

"Then why does this bother you so much?"

"Because somebody broke into his house. Probably somebody sent by someone I saw with my own eyes. The guy at the auction."

Dad snorted.

All he did was make me more indignant than before. "You weren't there. He could've been one of these people from those message boards, convinced the desk held the key to Una's death."

"It still has nothing to do with you." Dad must've considered the steaks ready since he brought them over to the table.

Holly got up and pulled out the baked potatoes. "Frankly, and you know I don't like sticking my nose into things, but I think your father's right. Haven't you been through enough already?" The fact that we happened to be in her kitchen when she asked that, the kitchen that had nearly been destroyed, wasn't lost on me.

For some reason, that was what it took. That was what got me thinking clearly again, along with the weight of a happy, healthy baby in my lap. "You're right. It's not my business. And if somebody wants to profit somehow from the diary—if that's what they found—that's up to them. Frankly, I would like to go back to when I didn't know Max Greene existed."

"I wonder if there's something we could do or say that would take your mind off it." The look Dad exchanged with Holly wasn't lost on me, not even a little bit.

"What's up?" My head swung back and forth between them. "Are you having another baby?"

Holly burst out laughing. "Please! Give me a break! I can barely handle him and my work and this one over here as it is." She nodded toward Dad, who pretended to be insulted.

"So what is it?" The two of them had been big on surprises lately. I looked down at the baby. "Do you know?"

"He does, but that's the thing about telling a baby a secret. You know he won't tell anybody." Holly giggled before reaching across the table. I put my hand in hers and she held it tight. "I decided I want you and Emma to be my maid of honor and matron of honor, respectively. If that would be okay with you."

It was like magic. All of a sudden, I didn't care about anything to do with Max or the desk for the diary or Una Howell herself.

"Really?" I might have squealed a little.

"Really. It would mean a lot to me." She and Dad exchanged a smile. "We decided we want to keep things simple. There's no reason for a big blowout wedding. Your dad and I have been together for a while already, we've settled our household, and now we have this little guy here." She blew a kiss to the baby. "What matters most is having people we love around us while we make it official. I would be honored to have the two of you up there with me."

I tried to hold back my emotion. I really did, if only to keep Georgie from sensing it and wailing.

It was no use. After railing against the relationship for so long and—I was sure—making things none too comfortable for Holly, she wanted to put all that aside. This was what I now realized I'd hoped for deep down in my heart, that she would forgive me and understand how badly I wanted to make it up to her.

"Well?" Dad beamed from ear to ear, looking every

inch the proud father. "What do you say? Will you stand up there with Holly and me?"

That did it. That was what broke the dam. Dinner sat forgotten for a bit while I sobbed my heart out.

And it was just what I needed.

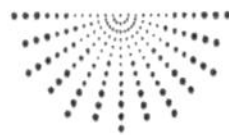

CHAPTER ELEVEN

"Of course, Emma totally lost it. Then Joe freaked out because he didn't know why Emma was losing it." I had to laugh at the memory. "I told Dad it would've been better if Holly asked her in person, but he was so excited. I think he was more excited than any of us, come to think of it."

"That is so sweet. I'm sure it makes him really happy to know his girls have accepted her."

Becca was right. To think, I was always so concerned with him, his health, all of that. I always wanted to do what was best for him, for my entire family. Sometimes, all it took was acceptance. Once we'd accepted the fact that Holly wasn't going anywhere and resenting her would never make things better, we had made his life much sweeter and easier.

Becca looked at the wall that stood between my store and Mom's café. "How is she taking it?"

"Surprisingly well. It's bonkers. I expected her to have one of those big, emotional scenes. Honestly, I was afraid it might set her back a little bit. She's come a long way since those first days—first years, even."

"Time heals just about everything, I guess." Becca checked her phone and frowned a little before sliding it back in her pocket.

I couldn't help but say something. "What's up? That's not the first time today you checked your phone. Are you waiting for something?"

She slid me a guilty look. "Sorry. I'm a little distracted."

"What's up?"

Her face worked like she wanted to fess up, but didn't. She was arguing with herself. I decided to give her space. I would be there for her if she wanted me to be.

Finally, it burst out of her. "Max said he would call me and he didn't. I keep hoping to at least get a text telling me he was busy or something." Her chin quivered a little bit at the end, which had the effect of a bomb going off in my head.

There was no holding my tongue anymore. "He's a

jerk. I'm sorry, but it's true. I know you like him, but—"

She shook her head hard. "No, I was silly. I let myself get all swept up because I like his work so much."

"And he's pretty cute." Even I had to admit that. "And he has that whole charm thing going on."

"You're telling me. Still, I fell for it. Hook, line and sinker. We never even went out on a date, and I'm standing here with a broken heart."

"Oh, sweetie, I'm sorry." I gave her a big hug while mentally cursing Max. Sure, we might've done a lot of business thanks to his appearance in the store, but was that worth all the trouble he put us through? "Do you need anything? How about I duck next door and grab you a treat? I know food isn't the answer, but some-times it feels like it is."

That got her giggling, anyway. "I already did that this morning before coming over here. I think I ate two blueberry muffins in roughly twenty seconds."

"That sounds about right. I've gone through almost an entire pan on my worst days. It doesn't help that they're so darned delicious."

She giggled again, which was good. She would get over this in time—like she said, it healed just about everything. As far as I was concerned, I never wanted to hear Max Greene's name again, and once we finished selling out of the books we'd ordered with the signing in mind, I didn't intend to restock them.

Funny how fate seemed to have other plans.

The front door burst open, making the bell above it jangle. My heart sank. *Speak of the devil.*

Max ripped off his sunglasses before plastering himself against the wall between the front door and the front window. He peeked out, then ducked back again. Meanwhile, Becca and I stood in mute wonder. He hadn't even said hello.

"What are you doing here?" I had to know.

He only waved a hand like I was a pest, still looking out the window. Becca and I exchanged a look.

I bit back some of my irritation. Some of it. "Hello?"

"Just wait a second." He craned his neck, looking out one more time, and heaved a sigh. "I'm sorry. I feel like I went to sleep on Friday night and woke up in a thriller."

"What are you talking about?" Whatever it was, he took it very seriously. There was a drawn look to him, circles under his eyes, and he hadn't bothered shaving in at least the past two days. Considering he mentioned Friday night and this was Sunday morning, it checked out. I still had no idea why.

He rubbed his temples, his eyes closing. "I'm sorry. Really, I'm not usually this dramatic." I had my doubts, but was willing to accept this. "Somebody's been following me. I was hoping to hang around town a little, to get an idea of where the police are with the case. And I'm starting to think I signed my death warrant."

Even Becca looked skeptical, and maybe a little annoyed. "Your death warrant? Did somebody take a shot at you?"

I expected him to shoot her a withering look, but he seemed to take the question seriously. "No. Somebody has been following me around, like I said. I can't go anywhere without this gray BMW on my tail. At first I thought I was making it up. You know, tricking myself into thinking there was more to the break-in at Ethan's than there actually was. But now I'm not so sure."

He ran a hand through his hair, and I noticed that hand was shaking. Whether he was truly being followed or not, he believed he was. That in itself was a reason for me to wheel out the chair from my office and have him take a seat. Becca offered to go next door and grab him some water. We exchanged a worried look before she ducked out.

I didn't know what to do. How was I supposed to handle this? And why in the world had he come to me? I decided to ask that question first.

He looked up at me, blinking like I'd asked the stupidest question in the world. "I wanted to come in and apologize to Becca for not calling her before now. I've been so distracted by this car following me wherever I go. I don't want to go home at this rate. I wouldn't want somebody following me there."

"I didn't realize you were still in town."

"I didn't want to leave with so much up in the air, so I got a room at one of the hotels on the beach." He blew out a frustrated sigh. "Here I was, thinking the police might be able to track down the thief who stole what belongs to me. If nothing else, I would like to get the money back for the desk. Almost five grand down the drain, and all I have is a banged-up piece of furniture. They should pay for the damage, whoever they are."

"I know the police are still working on it." Though Dad's less-than-positive take on the case tickled the back of my mind. Whoever did it would likely never be found. He wore gloves, nobody had seen him except for Ethan and even then, he didn't get a good look at the person. There was very little to do in a situation like this.

Max snorted. "A lot of good it's doing me. I'm sure this thief is bolder than ever. He thinks he can get away with anything."

I bit the inside of my cheek because, frankly, the melodrama was starting to go over the top. "There's no reason for him to follow you around, though. Or to hurt you. Right?"

"How do I know?" He threw his hands into the air before letting them drop into his lap. "I never would've imagined anyone would know about the diary, either. The hidden drawer, any of it. Yet here I am. It's enough to make me question everything I thought I knew." He rubbed his temples again, his eyes sliding shut.

It was a relief when Becca came in—at least, until I saw the look on her face. "Okay, I'm not trying to make things worse, but a gray BMW definitely drove by as I was coming out of the café."

"See?" Max's eyes bulged, bloodshot and full of fear. "I'm telling you, somebody is following me. And I have no idea why." I knew Becca would never make up something like that. She wouldn't even mention it unless she was sure what she'd seen. I stood by the window, staring out onto a very calm Main Street while Becca did what she could to calm Max down. I pretended not to hear when he offered a murmured apology for not having called, too.

Still, I didn't know whether to be glad or not. All he was doing was making her like him again. It wasn't my place to say anything, though.

Once it seemed like their private conversation was over, I turned back toward them. "Well, we can call over to the station. I'm sure they would be glad to send someone over to talk with you about this."

His expression brought to mind a grate sliding over a storefront. "Absolutely not." He was so stony, so adamant, it took my breath away.

"Why not?"

"Because I was over there earlier and they treated me like a child. I'm surprised none of them patted me on the head and gave me a cookie before sending me on my way." The disgust practically dripped from his voice.

"Sometimes that's the way it goes."

Becca shot me a horrified, guilty expression, but she really didn't need to. I knew what it felt like. The sense that nobody was listening, like nobody was taking me seriously. Granted, in his case, I could sort of understand why they would treat him that way.

I pursed my lips. "This is different. Somebody is

following you around. Did you catch any of the license plate?"

"No, and I could kick myself for it. I would tell you I'll take note of that next time, but I'm sort of hoping next time never comes." He cracked open the water bottle and downed a lot of it at once. "I'm sorry, but you have to understand. All the research I do, all the cases I examine? I can't help but feel paranoid. You know how many people brush situations like this off as *just one of those things*? Nothing to be worried about? They always end up regretting it in the end." Boy, was he a ray of sunshine.

Even so, he had a point. I could tell Becca thought so, too, judging by the way she chewed her lip while glancing time and again toward the window. She was more familiar with crime and unsolved cases than I was, so I could imagine how worried she must've felt.

He pulled out his phone. "I'm going to call Ethan and see if I can stay with him for a few days."

A big, red stop sign appeared in my mind's eye. "Are you sure that's a good idea?"

"Well, I'm not going home."

"But…" I glanced at Becca, who cringed in understanding. "Isn't that the same as sort of inviting trouble to his place? Again?"

"Oh, let's not start that again, please."

"I'm just saying. It strikes me is sort of unfair."

"Ethan is a big boy. He can make his own decisions."

I was so angry on Ethan's behalf, it wasn't even funny. "At least text him rather than calling. He's always really busy during the day."

"Good point. I'll do that. I don't know what I'm going to do while I wait for him to get back to me." Something told me we were going to have a guest at the store for a while. What did I do to deserve this?

"Oh, is that the desk?" Becca leaned in while Max typed out a message.

"Right, Ethan sent you those pictures, didn't he?" I joined Becca, peering at the screen. "Yeah, that's the one, the second picture he sent." Max tapped on the picture to enlarge it to full-screen.

I gasped, gripping Becca's shoulder. "That's him! The guy standing off to the side, the one wearing glasses. That's the one who kept counter-bidding. I'm sure of it!"

"Him?" Max enlarge the picture more, focusing on the man who just happened to be at the edge of the shot.

"Sure, he was practically guarding the desk before bidding even started."

Max pulled the phone up close to his face before

muttering something obscene. "You have got to be kidding me."

"What is it?"

"I know exactly who that is. And now everything makes sense." He jumped up from the chair, almost snarling as he stared at his screen. "I'm going to kill him."

CHAPTER TWELVE

"Let me get this straight." Ethan took a drink from his beer bottle before casting a grim look at his cousin. "The guy from the auction is another author in the same genre you write in."

"He hasn't had a success in a while. But yes." Max held up his phone to show off the photo he'd been staring daggers at all day. "Brian Mills. I would know him anywhere."

"And you assume because he was so interested in the desk that he also came to the conclusion the diary had to be in there."

"It's the only thing that makes sense! Now, every-thing's coming together. He must've done his research the way I did. He must've come to the same conclu-sions I did. No wonder he was so desperate to get his hands on it." Max snickered. "And that explains why he couldn't afford to outbid you that one last time. I can't imagine he's making much money from his backlist right now."

If we hadn't been in my apartment, I might've thrown something at him. I didn't feel like cleaning up the mess. It was strange—not many people stirred up that sort of reaction in me. Ethan had a way of stretching my patience to the breaking point, but I had never imagined literally throwing something heavy at him. "You sound a little smug."

"It's not my fault he can't write a good book anymore." Another snicker. "He probably thought he hit the mother lode. And now he's walking around with a diary that technically belongs to me."

"You don't know that for sure. Like I said, the man leaving my house looked nothing like him." Ethan pulled up the pictures on his own phone, shaking his head as he studied the one in question. "No, he was much leaner. Almost wiry. Nothing like this guy."

"Who knows? He could've had somebody do it for him. I'm telling you, no matter who actually went through with breaking into your house, he was the person who sent them there. I am absolutely sure of it now."

Meanwhile, I couldn't help but think this was all a

big coincidence. "You think he would go to all that trouble? For a diary, I mean?"

To say the man looked at me like I was the world's biggest rube would be fairly accurate. "It would be the key to everything."

"Assuming Una was murdered in the first place, which we still don't know one way or another."

He sat up a little straighter. "It's obvious you haven't done the kind of research I have."

"No, I haven't. You're right." Because while I didn't have much of a life, I did have better things to do than spend my free time obsessing over dead strangers. "And listen, would it surprise me if Una was murdered? No. People have been murdered for all kinds of reasons."

He smirked. "Right. Because you're personally experienced with things like this."

"More than you are, I'd bet." Though I would've been glad to give him a little personal experience then and there. The arrogant creep. "I have first-hand knowledge of how people act when they're cornered, when they're desperate. You've read about it and written stories."

"Okay, enough." Ethan shook his head only once, his eyes on me.

Somehow that only made the burning anger in my

chest hotter and harder to ignore. The fact that he, of all people, acted like the voice of reason. It had the effect of pouring gasoline on a fire.

He stood in front of Max, arms folded. "You need to be a little more respectful. Darcy was nice enough to let you skulk around her store all day so you could hide from this supposed stalker you're so worried about. And now we're here at her apartment. I wouldn't stand in the way if she decided to kick you out."

I silently rejoiced as Max shrank back a little. "Fine. Sorry." I decided it was better to keep my mouth shut rather than comment on how immature and petulant he seemed—even though my blood was simmering, I had the self-awareness to know I'd be just as bad as him if I smarted off.

Besides, I didn't much love the thought of being reprimanded again. I could take it from anybody but Ethan.

"Okay. Where does this leave us?" Ethan sat on the sofa, near where his cousin sat in the armchair. I had to wonder whether that was to keep Max from starting trouble, or to keep my hands from finding Max's throat. "We know the other bidder was this writer who may or may not have been interested in

Una's untimely death." Though he snickered a little around the word *untimely*.

"I say we go to his house and demand the diary." Max had the audacity to look surprised when Ethan and I stared at him, open-mouthed. "What? Let's get it over with."

"I can't speak for Darcy, but it's your use of words like *we* that has me a little confused." Ethan looked at me for confirmation.

I nodded, though deep down inside I couldn't pretend to be completely turned off by Max's suggestion. Did make me a hypocrite, wanting more than anything to talk to this Brian person but pretending I thought it was a terrible idea? Of course, it did. That didn't stop me.

Max scowled. "You're not going to send me on my own, are you?"

"I'm not sending you anywhere."

"You know what I mean. If this is ever going to come to an end, the man has to be dealt with in person. If he's desperate enough to break into your house while you were there, and then to follow me around town, I don't think it would be wise for me to go by myself."

"Who says you have to go at all?"

"I do. Because if he stole something from my property, it's mine."

I had to satisfy my curiosity. "Do you know this Brian? I mean, personally? Or is it more a matter of, you know, somebody whose work you're familiar with?"

"What difference does it make?"

Just as obstinate as his cousin. No question whether or not they came from the same family.

I sighed. "It makes a difference because this guy might be really unhinged, for all you know. It might be better for your safety to leave it alone."

Ethan managed to stop himself before he laughed out loud, but a couple soft snickers slipped through.

I was unstoppable at this point, though. "Yes, I know I'm hardly one to talk. But I'm trying to learn from my mistakes, and I would hate to see somebody walk right into the kind of situation I would normally walk into and end up regretting it later." Even if, frankly, Max could waltz into a sticky situation with his eyes wide open and I would gladly wave goodbye.

"Good point." Ethan turned to Max. "I know you don't want to hear this, but I have to say it. It's one thing to research and to write about cases like this. It's another thing to get mixed up in real life. And this is real-life stuff we're talking about. If you don't know anything about this Brian Mills, there's no telling what we're walking into." He used the word *we*. What a pushover. I made a mental note to tease him later.

"What if you took this to the police?" I suggested, then glared at Ethan, whose mouth was falling open. "What? Why is that such a crazy idea?"

"It's just that I'm wondering who you are and where the real Darcy is."

I stuck my tongue out. "I'm serious. I'm sure if you talked to Pete Frazer and told him about all of this, he would be willing to go with you. He might even tell you to stay put while he did it himself."

"A lot of good that will do. What, do you honestly think a desperate author who finally got his hands on the key to unlocking his next bestseller will crumple because some small-town cop knocks on his door?"

"But he will because you knocked on the door?" I scratched my head. "That doesn't make much sense. I would think police presence would make it more likely for him to fold and hand it over."

Ethan grunted. "She's right."

"I'm not involving the police." When I rolled my eyes, Max mimicked me with an eye roll of his own. "I'm not."

"Why not? If you feel like someone is threatening you, and you feel like this might be the person doing it, and now we have reason to believe Brian Mills might be the one behind all of this, why wouldn't you want to involve the police?" It made no sense to me. The man was more of an enigma than Ethan, which was saying something.

Ethan emptied his bottle, then used it to point at his cousin as he got up and went to the kitchen. "I think I know why."

"I'm all ears." I glanced at Max, but his face was unreadable.

"He doesn't want to involve the police because he doesn't want the police to end up solving Una's murder—if it was a murder." Ethan leaned against the kitchen doorway, arms folded, a smile spreading as Max avoided his gaze, then looked at the floor.

I scowled. "You're kidding. Is he right?" Max hunched his shoulders, like he was retreating into a shell the way a turtle would. "I cannot believe this. That's all you care about?"

"It's my work." He scoffed, but it was a weak attempt. His heart wasn't in it. "You wouldn't know about that."

"Oh, please, spare me the tortured artist act. Okay? We're talking about real life here. And let me tell you something." I went to him, crouching when he wouldn't lift his head to look at me. Our eyes finally met. "You weren't thinking about your work when you came running into my store today. You were thinking about how afraid you are for your life. Can you honestly tell me it's more important for you to be the first person to break this case, without any sort of police involvement? More important than your life?"

"Yes." He almost jumped up from his chair, moving so abruptly I nearly fell over in surprise. "I'm going. I know where he lives."

"How do you know where he lives?"

"We had the same publisher for a little while. He threw a big party at his house back in the day for his last release. That must've been three, maybe four years ago, but I remember the house. It's in North Jersey, one of those obnoxious McMansions. Close enough to the city that he liked to tell people he lived there—and once pressed for details, he would admit he lived across the river." He snickered, scrolling through contacts on his phone. "Here it is. I stored the address."

"Don't do this." Ethan went so far as to stand in front of my door, blocking his cousin's progress. "This is crazy."

"You're going to have to get out of my way." Max jerked a thumb toward the second door, the one leading to the stairs running along the side of the house. "You know I can get out that way, too, right?"

"Darcy can block the back door." Yes, but there was one problem. Darcy did not feel like blocking the door. As far as Darcy was concerned, Max could leave and never come back and she—I, rather—would not have cared very much. I might even have thrown a small party.

"I'm going to go, regardless of what you think." Max fell back a step. "Unless you want to come with me. That way, you can make sure everything is on the up and up."

Suddenly, I had the feeling that was exactly what Max wanted all along. And Ethan had played right into his hands.

One thing was for sure. I wasn't about to let them go without me.

Even if that made me no better than Max.

CHAPTER THIRTEEN

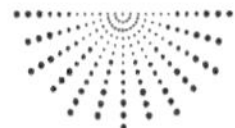

"I would feel a lot better about this if Pete or Joe or somebody was with us." Of course, my words fell on deaf ears.

I might as well have been talking to myself. After all, nobody cared that I thought it would've been better to wait until morning to make this little trip up the Parkway. It was nearly eight o'clock by the time we hit the road, meaning it would be at least ten when we reached our destination. At least traffic wasn't very heavy at this time of night. I hoped that would help.

"Maybe it would've been better if you had stayed home." Ethan shot me a look from the corner of his eye. "We don't know what we're going to find when we get there."

"Please. Like I would pass up the opportunity to watch this unfold."

Meanwhile, Max sat in the backseat, typing frantically on his laptop. I could only hope he wasn't documenting every moment of our journey—and that if he was, he would be kind toward me. I didn't much love the idea of reading unflattering things about myself.

I'd always heard jokes about people being nice to the writers in their life, and now I understood where those jokes came from. Nobody wanted to end up reading all about their gory murder.

Especially if they had a tendency toward bickering with the author.

At least the ride would pass quickly, with Ethan entering Brian's neighborhood short of ten o'clock. I couldn't help but whistle in appreciation of the houses we passed on the quiet, perfectly maintained street. "I thought you said he's been down on his luck these past few years."

"He has. If I remember correctly from that party, he told everybody he paid for the house in full."

I turned toward him in surprise. "He made that much money?"

In the light from the laptop, I watched Max grimace in obvious distaste. "His last book was the third in a line of extremely successful projects. The first one sold like gangbusters, the second I did better than that. Of course, his agent used that success to broker a massive advance on the third book—which earned out in no time." Boy, was he jealous. I could practically taste his envy.

"It's a shame he hasn't had much luck these past few years."

Ethan murmured his agreement. "And I'm sure the taxes out here are no joke, not to mention the maintenance on homes this big."

"Which is all the more reason for him to do something desperate. Do you see why I'm so sure about this?"

Ethan and I stayed silent, but we shared a look that told me he and I were on the same page. I still thought this was way too thin of a theory.

"I don't think this is a good idea." Yes, there were lights on in the house, now visible thanks to Ethan turning into the driveway. From the street, the house was hidden from view behind a stone wall. The driveway curved on the way to the house, trees lining both sides, with what looked like solar lights providing a little illumination. It was very pretty, well-maintained, and it gave me hope that Brian wasn't the poor, hapless loser Max made him out to be.

Max snorted. "You didn't have to come."

"That's not what I meant." I turned around. "It's late. He might be in bed. Nobody wants three strangers pulling up to their house at ten o'clock, not for any reason."

"But I'm not a stranger." Max waited until Ethan put the car in park in front of the house, then bolted from the back seat. Ethan and I scrambled to catch up to him, meeting him at the front door by the time he jammed his finger against the bell.

"We don't even know if he lives here anymore. Did you ever think of that?" Ethan nudged Max. "I can't believe I went along with this. All to keep you from getting yourself killed."

Max didn't have the chance to answer before a voice came from a speaker above the doorbell. "What do you want? Do you know what time it is?" I looked at Ethan, and the slight widening of his eyes told me he recognized the voice, too. This was the man from the auction—slightly breathy, a little congested.

"Brian Mills? I want what you stole from me." Max leaned in a little, staring at what I now understood was a doorbell cam. "Open the door and stop being a coward."

There was a moment of silence, and in that moment I sincerely wished I could dissolve into the brick patio. I wondered if he recognized us. I almost wanted to tell him I had nothing to do with this crazy scheme but, facts were facts. I couldn't magically remove myself from the scene.

"Max Greene?" Brian's laugh was full of obvious distaste. "What are you doing here? What do you think I took from you?"

"You know what you took from me."

"I'm pretty sure I don't since I've never taken anything from you. I don't even want anything of yours."

"You had nothing to do with the vandalization of a certain desk you lost at auction?"

More silence. This was getting us nowhere. I nudged Max aside and leaned in. "Mr. Mills, we're so sorry to disturb you tonight. I don't know if you remember me from the auction, but my friend here was bidding on that desk that belonged to Una Howell? The two of you sort of went back and forth over it?"

"Oh, it's you." Brian snickered. "Sure, I remember. I still don't quite understand what any of this is about, though."

"Can you please let us in? I'm sure we can explain. Or if it would make you feel better, you could come out here." Max inhaled like he was about to speak, so I accidentally-on-purpose stepped on his foot to shut him up. "We are so sorry for disturbing you, really. But things have gotten a little hairy, and we wanted to eliminate you as a possible suspect."

Meanwhile, Ethan tapped me on the shoulder. I followed the direction of his gaze and found another car in the driveway besides his. There was a white Toyota sitting there, in good condition but in a completely different league from a BMW. No, it didn't necessarily mean anything, the man could have had another car, but this was one more piece of the puzzle.

And the puzzle didn't seem to point to Brian as our man.

"Get out here, Mills. Stop being a coward." Max hammered the door with the side of his fist.

"Would you stop? For heaven's sake." I pointed to Ethan's vehicle. "You can wait in the car if you don't know how to behave yourself."

The sound of soft laughter coming from the speaker drew our attention. "All right. Only because of the girl." I didn't know how I felt about being called *the girl,* but if it meant getting to the bottom of this, I could overlook it. The three of us stepped back from the door, waiting, and it was less than a minute before the door opened and I found myself face-to-face with the man from the auction. Mr. Glasses himself.

I thrust out my hand before Max could say

anything insulting. "My name is Darcy Harmon. It's nice to meet you. This is Ethan Crosby." The men nodded to each other before Brian turned his attention on Max. I recognized the narrowing of his eyes behind his glasses, the firm set of his thin mouth.

"So why are you here? I was about to turn in for the night."

Max barked out a disbelieving laugh. "You know why I'm here. Where is it?"

"Where's what?"

"Don't play games with me. I know you broke into my cousin's house. You paid somebody to do it for you."

"Excuse me?" Brian looked at Ethan while running a hand over his thinning, brown hair. "What's he talking about?"

Ethan thrust his hands into his pockets, where they tightened into fists. "Someone broke into my house. The night of the auction, after the desk was dropped off there. I came out of the shower to find someone had smashed one of the drawers on the floor. They almost tore the desk apart looking for something."

As Ethan spoke, I watched Brian's face. Was I an expert in reading body language and expressions? No, but I wasn't bad, either. I looked for a hint of recognition, understanding. Guilt.

What I saw instead surprised me, though it shouldn't have. After all, I had already spent far too much time with Max, but then that didn't mean all true crime authors were as wacky as he was. Or as obsessed.

I was wrong, at least about this one. "What did they find? Did they find anything?" The man was almost salivating, trembling from the intensity of his reaction.

"You know very well what they found, so stop lying! This is pathetic." Max threw his arms in the air. "You know what was in that desk just as much as I do, which is the only reason you cared as much as you did about the auction. And when you lost, you decided to take what you wanted."

Brian took a deep breath. I could practically hear him counting to ten in his head. His face went from bright red to a slightly less alarming shade. "I didn't do anything. I drove back up here after the auction and went to dinner in the city with a few friends. I paid, and I have the receipt. I'd be happy to get it for you, along with the record of my E-ZPass activity. See, alibi. That's what we call that." He sported an expression of superiority.

I glanced at Ethan, whom I found watching me. He lifted a shoulder along with an eyebrow. I didn't believe Brian had anything to do with it, but then I never really had. Seeing him again, speaking to him, observing his reaction when he heard about the burglary… none of it pointed to him being the one.

Max, of course, had other ideas. "Like you couldn't have paid somebody to do it for you." He jerked a thumb toward Ethan. "He already said the guy looked nothing like you, and I wouldn't be surprised if you made sure to have records to prove you were all the way up here that night."

If I were Brian, I would've kicked us off the property by that point. It was all such a mistake. An embarrassing one, at that.

Instead of telling us to go pound sand, however, he let out a gleeful little snort. "I've gotta admit, it's sort of fun, knowing you think I'm some criminal genius or whatever. You honestly think I'd go to those lengths? Why would I do that?"

"To confirm whether Una was murdered and write a book about the case, obviously."

"Hmm. Not a bad idea." Brian folded his arms over a Simpsons t-shirt that looked like it might've been through a hundred washings. "It'd mean breaking the case wide open. The murderinos would go nuts."

"Murderinos?" I had never heard that one before.

"Not a nice name, but one used to describe people interested in murder—especially unsolved murders."

Brian's gaze remained fixed on Max. "And you think I'd go so far as to hire a burglar, too? Where do you think I'd get the money for that?"

"You were ready to pay a small fortune for the desk."

That was a good point. I watched Brian, waiting for his answer.

He swallowed hard, his lashes fluttering. "I would've had to spread the amount across a couple credit cards, if you must know." Finally, his head fell back, and a groan filled the air. "Okay. Yeah. I wanted the desk because I figured it'd be the perfect hiding place for a diary. It was a gamble. I was willing to make it."

We remained silent.

Then he pointed at Max. "But you're dead wrong if you think I'd scheme to get my hands on it anyway. Fair's fair. I didn't win the desk." He looked at Ethan next. "If anything, I was hoping I could get in touch with you and explain why I was so interested. I was hoping we could work something out, like a co-writing credit or something."

"So you did want to write a book!" Max practically bounced up and down, gleeful. "I knew it! You haven't had a release in years and your brand is non-existent now. It's obvious."

I winced. Ethan covered his face with his hand.

Brian, however, only smiled. "Not that you're entitled to know before the rest of the world does, but the details of my latest deal are due to come out in the next *Publisher's Weekly*. I believe the word they'll use to describe it is *significant*." He then looked my way. "That means I'm getting a lot of money."

"That's great news!" I tried to make my smile genuine. It sort of was. Sort of.

And it almost totally blew Max's theory out of the water. Brian might've hit a dry patch in his career, but things were looking up—without Una Howell.

"And you can't pretend I did it to screw you over, either, since I had no idea this guy was your cousin." Brian inclined his head toward Ethan. "I didn't know you had anything to do with it. It would've been great to get my hands on the diary, but I'm not some desperate thief. Sorry you had to come all this way to find that out." He neither looked nor sounded sorry, and I couldn't blame him.

Ethan slung an arm around Max's shoulders and forced a smile that verged on being scary. "Thank you for your time. I'm sorry we bothered you. We'll be going now." When Max's mouth fell open, Ethan's arm tightened. He steered Max toward the car while I mumbled apologies before hurrying behind them.

"Is that enough for you?" Ethan opened the back door and shoved his cousin inside. "Or do you want to waste another four hours on yet another dead end?"

Max folded his arms, scowling, neither speaking nor looking at either of us. I slid into the passenger seat and deliberately avoided looking at him. I was afraid he'd bite my head off.

And I did feel slightly sorry for him. Nobody wanted to be embarrassed like that.

The ride home was almost painfully quiet. At least we made good time.

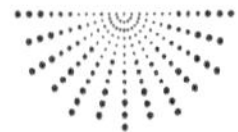

CHAPTER FOURTEEN

"Is there anybody else it could've been?"

I rolled my eyes at my sister, who sat with her feet up on one of the chairs in the café. "You're a lot of help. I'm standing here, telling you I want to drop the entire thing like a bad habit, and you're speculating on who could've done it."

"Just because it wasn't that Brian guy doesn't mean you have to stop trying to find who did it."

"Enough, please." Mom gave us both a stern look. "You're only encouraging your sister to take risks. You're a bad influence."

I stuck out my tongue, and Emma did the same.

Mom patted my shoulder on her way back to the kitchen. The café was due to open in another twenty minutes or so and she was in a hurry as always to get things ready for her faithful customers. "You're smart to want to put this behind you, sweetheart. I only wish your sister had as much sense when she was running around, sticking her nose where it didn't belong."

"I know. I've always been the good one." I grinned at Emma, who made a sour face.

The second Mom was out of earshot, however, new light flickered behind her eyes. "You know what you should do?"

"Mind my own business?"

"See if you can find the housekeeper. Una's, I mean."

"Well, I didn't think you meant mine." I did everything I could to seem uninterested as I pulled chairs from on top of the other tables and set them up.

"Have you looked her up?"

"I don't even know her name."

"I bet Becca would know it. Probably right off the top of her head." When I frowned, she got insistent. "Tell me you don't think she's been combing those message boards for everything Una-related."

She had a point. "To what end, though? I'm sure the poor woman wants to live the rest of her life in peace. She wasn't even there when Una died. And I'll bet she feels bad about it."

"Unless she was behind it."

"Oh, come on." I set down the last chair with a thump. "You're reaching now."

"And you've never done that?" She deliberately looked away from the platter of brownies Mom carried out from the kitchen, unable to even see them without getting emotional because she wasn't supposed to be eating them.

"Never done what?" Mom looked at me, then at Emma. "What am I missing?"

"Your younger daughter trying to convince your firstborn to do something gross."

"Not gross. Completely reasonable, I think. Asking the housekeeper whether Una was hanging around the wrong people." She placed her feet on the floor, her swollen ankles forgotten. "Or maybe some estranged relative was sniffing around. Maybe they came to the house and caused trouble and Una threw them out."

"You're getting ahead of yourself." It was a waste of time. I knew better than to dissuade my sister once she got on a roll.

Mom, on the other hand, had no problems with it. "Now stop this immediately. I'm serious. I don't want to hear another thing about it."

We both froze, eyes wide. Mom was no stranger to getting sharp with us when she felt sharpness was needed, but this was a little intense even for her.

"I'm sorry." Emma truly looked and sounded sorry, too.

"So am I." There I was, feeling like a naughty kid being chastised for something that wasn't really my fault. What was I supposed to do, though? Tattle on my sister? Blame it on her?

Mom shook her head, her laugh tight and forced. "Sorry. I'm a little on edge, I guess."

"What's going on?" I put an arm around her shoulders. "You okay?"

"I'm fine. I'm tired of worrying about you girls, is all. I wish you would leave well enough alone. Both of you." She scowled at Emma. "You're about to be a mother in a few months. Doesn't that mean anything? And this one's supposed to be the baby's godmother." She elbowed me, which made me regret our current proximity.

"You're right. As always." Though my sister hardly looked like she meant it. She'd always been a pro at saying one thing while she meant the complete opposite. One talent I'd always wished I had a little of, since my face was so easy to read. At least according to Pete.

It was better to change the subject. I asked about Bob and whether they'd done anything together on Sunday night rather than pursue things further. She seemed to cheer up, so at least I'd done one thing right.

Though Emma wasn't about to be put off that easily. Once Frankie arrived and got ready to serve some coffee and baked goodies, I headed over to the store with my sister on my heels. There was no need to ask what she was so enthused about, either. "I'm telling you. Look up the housekeeper."

"You're driving me crazy." I unlocked and opened the door to the store—where the sight of Becca already dusting shelves made me yelp in surprise. I put a hand over my chest, where my heart raced out of control.

"Sorry, sorry." Becca waved to Emma. "I didn't mean to scare you."

Once I regained the ability to speak, I asked the most obvious question. "What are you doing here so early?"

"I wanted to make sure the store was tidied up."

I couldn't help but narrow my eyes in disbelief. "You were here yesterday and it looked just fine when we left." With Max. I now knew exactly what this was about.

"Fine." She dropped the dust rag. "I've been dying to know what happened after you went home. Of all the times for me to have to babysit my nephew."

"Believe me. You had more fun than I did." I filled her in while Emma took a seat behind the counter and made it quite clear through her grunts, snickers and tongue clicks just how she felt about the story.

"So it wasn't that other author, after all." Becca sounded about as disappointed as Max had been the entire way home.

Emma's hand shot into the air. "I have a theory."

I spun on my heel and glared at her. "You shush."

Too late. "What is it?" Becca very clearly held her breath, teeth sinking into her lip.

I was outnumbered. "She wants us to look up the housekeeper."

"Oh! Julia Lewis? I know where to find her."

I should've known. "This isn't a good idea." Talk about a waste of breath. They were already talking over me, with Becca giving Emma the details of Julia's care facility.

"She's been there for around a year, if I remember correctly." Becca whipped out her phone and did a little tapping, then nodded. "Yeah, according to this, she moved in with her son for a little while but things didn't work out, so she moved to this new place."

She lowered the phone, lips pursed, brow furrowed. "Una provided for her in her will. Generously."

"Is that only rumor? Or is it a fact?" I watched over Becca's shoulder as she pulled up a site for the facility Julia called home. One look at the place answered my question.

Una had provided for her. Generously. "Holy moly, it looks like a spa."

"And it's only an hour from here." Becca eyed me, mouth clamped shut.

She didn't need to say a word.

"No way."

"We could be back before lunch! We don't even open for another hour."

"Great. But we do have to open and allow customers to come in, right?"

Emma's hand shot up again. "I'd be more than happy to fill in while you're gone."

"You're so generous. And lucky to be carrying a child right now, because otherwise I'd have to kill you for starting this in the first place."

Becca laughed. "Please. I've been wanting to talk to Julia for ages. Everybody has."

"So… if everybody knows where she lives, why hasn't everybody already gone to see her?" I folded my arms and might have acted slightly smug.

"Maybe they won't let any random people in there, which makes sense." Emma tapped her chin while wearing an expression I knew too well. "I wonder what you could say to get in."

Becca, meanwhile, returned to the message boards. "Maybe there aren't enough locals to make it a big deal? Some of these accounts are posting from other countries, even." It blew my mind to imagine anybody on the other side of the world caring about a woman's life here in Cape Hope.

"There's only one way to find out." Emma tapped her fingers together under her chin, eyes dancing. "I'm more than happy to hang here until you get back."

"You're so generous." Why did I bother arguing at all? I should've known it was a lost cause from the get-go. "Do me a favor, though, okay? And this is just as much for me as it is for you."

She made an X over her chest. "If anybody tells Mom you're not here, I'll make up a story. She'll never find out."

That wasn't quite good enough. "What will you tell her?"

"What about… you went on a breakfast date? She'd love that."

I wasn't sure anymore whether the truth was more dangerous.

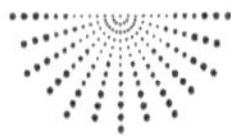

CHAPTER FIFTEEN

"Please, don't make me regret this." I adjusted my shirt and brushed invisible lint from my jeans. My knees were practically knocking together, while my eyes kept darting over to the beautiful brick building.

"What do you think could happen that'd make you regret doing this?"

"For starters, if Julia gets agitated and the administrator calls the police, this could eventually get back home. I'd never hear the end of it from Dad or Joe. Or Pete." Naturally, it was Pete I was most concerned with, mostly because I was used to hearing it from Dad and Joe was too busy obsessing over the baby to care much about what I did.

Besides, if my brother-in-law wanted to get an attitude, I'd tell him to take it to his wife. She was the reason for this nonsense.

"I'm sure that won't happen. We're both emotionally intelligent enough to manage this without upsetting her." Becca strode ahead of me like a woman on a mission. Her confidence was almost enough to make me feel confident, too. Almost.

"Good morning." She was all smiles for the crew behind the front desk, which was decorated tastefully but lavishly with lush floral arrangements all along the marble counter. "Sign here?" She pointed to the book lying open in front of us.

A cheerful girl nodded. "Who are you here to see?"

"Julia Lewis." Becca's smile never wavered. Meanwhile, my insides had somehow gotten the idea I was on a ship in the middle of a hurricane.

The girl blinked a few times before her smile widened. "I'm sure Mrs. Lewis will be happy to receive company. Can I… ask what this is about?"

When we both stared in mute horror, she cringed. "It's just that we've never seen either of you around here before. That's all. It's in the interest of our residents that we make sure they aren't harassed or otherwise bothered."

"Of course." I was as sympathetic as could be. "We're

from Julia's hometown. My father's a detective there and with the Howell auction that took place last week, he wondered how Mrs. Lewis is holding up. He always said she seemed devastated by Miss Howell's passing and felt awful for her. I was on my way through town and thought we could stop in to check up on her."

The girl bought it. Her expression softened. "That's very sweet. I'm sure she'll like to visit with people from Paradise City."

My head snapped back. "We're from Cape Hope."

She pointed at me, grinning. "That was a test. You passed. I'll show you to Mrs. Lewis's room." I could've fainted with relief. Becca gave me a discreet thumbs up before we set out down the hall.

The woman sitting near the window, crocheting while watching a morning game show on TV, looked up with a smile when we entered the spacious suite. The door to her bedroom was open, revealing even more space, and the bathroom looked like something out of an architectural magazine.

"Mrs. Lewis, you have visitors from back home!" The girl picked up a tray that looked like it used to hold breakfast. There was a beautiful teapot and matching cup and saucer still on it. I wondered if they had any open rooms available. I might not have looked the part, but I was usually in bed before ten and liked an early dinner whenever possible.

Julia put her crocheting aside. "Welcome, ladies. Please, have a seat." She looked so happy, her lined face lighting up as Becca and I sat on a floral printed sofa. Julia picked up the remote to turn down the volume on the TV, quieting the screaming audience and the contestant who'd just won a new car.

"Mrs. Lewis, it's such a pleasure to meet you." Becca's voice was strangely tight, like excitement made it tough to speak. I put a hand on her leg in hopes of reminding her to chill out.

"Please, call me Julia." She had a beautiful smile and a gentle voice. I had a tough time imagining her running a wealthy household, ordering staff around and overseeing things. Then again, being a leader didn't always mean being the loudest person in the room.

"This is a beautiful facility." I looked around, shaking my head in wonder. "My grandmother lived in an assisted living facility for a while and it was nowhere near as gorgeous as this."

"Yes, I know how lucky I am. Believe me." She nodded sagely, a solemn expression replacing her welcoming one. "Una provided well. A lot of people didn't like her much—she could be difficult—but they didn't know how generous and kind she was." There was heavy fondness in her voice.

I never could've imagined her leading us straight into the reason why we'd come to see her, but now that she'd already started in that direction, I couldn't see steering away from it. "You worked at the house for a long time, didn't you?"

"Most of my life. My mother was the cook, my father the gardener. Una saw to their retirement once her parents passed and she came into her money." Julia's pale blue eyes brimmed with tears. "They never forgot that, and neither did I."

"How sweet." Becca was still overwhelmed, so I plunged ahead. "I visited the house just a few days ago."

"The auction?" I nodded. "Yes, Lawrence told me about that."

"Lawrence?"

"Una's attorney." Her mouth screwed up in what looked like a disapproving scowl, and I made a note of it. "He sees to my money and makes sure the bills are paid for this place. He visited last week to check on me and informed me of the auction."

It didn't take a genius to figure out she wasn't a fan of the event. "I'm sorry you weren't able to be there for it, so you could see who got to take home all that beautiful furniture."

She lowered her brow, and I had no problem imagining her ruling over a huge house. All of a sudden I wanted to jump up and dust something. "Vultures. Picking at the bones."

"I'm so sorry you feel that way about it. I guess Lawrence didn't check in with you to see how you felt about it beforehand, huh?"

Her bony shoulders lifted under the sweater she wore. "I had no say in it, regardless. Though I would very much have liked to go back one last time, while the house looked the way I remember it. The way Lawrence made it sound, he left it as it was for all these years."

"It looked very much like it hadn't been touched, but it was still in excellent condition." I could tell that was the right thing to say when a look of relief came over her face.

"We worked so hard to maintain the house, to keep her from falling into disrepair. Many of the homes built around that time were allowed to rot."

"I've lived in Cape Hope all my life, so I know what you mean."

At that, she laughed merrily. "You can't be older than thirty, my dear."

"I'm just shy of that, actually." We laughed together. "Through rumor and legend, I mean. I understand some of the wealthier families died off and their descendants didn't have the money to even pay the taxes."

"Yes, time changes everything. But I do have my memories." She turned her head slightly, and I followed the direction of her gaze to a thick binder I soon realized was a photo album. Becca saw it, too, and I'd swear the girl was vibrating with excitement.

She cleared her throat. "Is that your photo album over there?"

"Yes. Would you like to look through it?" Julia was surprisingly spry for her age, popping up from her chair and hurrying over to the bookshelf. "No one ever asks to look through my pictures. It's been a while since I've opened this up." We gave her room on the sofa and she sat between us. The smell of lavender and vanilla clung to her, giving me a comfortable feeling. I hoped it would calm Becca down. Regardless of whether or not Julia could tell us anything about Una, she was a nice lady who didn't deserve to be agitated.

The photos themselves were gorgeous, but it was clear Julia had taken pains to make sure they stayed that way. She handled the pages with care, making sure she didn't touch any of the pictures themselves.

"This was a Fourth of July party back in… Oh, 1965, I believe. It was the first party at the house in many years. Mr. and Mrs. Howell didn't much enjoy big crowds and excitement. Mrs. Howell passed in sixty-four, and Mr. Howell followed her a few short months later. In a way, this was Una's coming-out party. She was finally able to run the estate as she wished."

"Is that her?" I leaned in to examine the image in front of me.

"Yes, wasn't she lovely? She would have been around your age at this time, I think."

She was lovely, tall and statuesque, with a brilliant smile and regal bearing. She'd worn a chic sheath dress that showed off her slim figure, and her dark hair was piled in countless curls and waves at the back of her head. I couldn't imagine how heavy it must've been.

It was her smile I kept coming back to.

"She was beautiful." There was a hushed awe in Becca's voice.

I tried to imagine what it must be like, seeing Una like this after thinking of her as an old woman for so long. This version of Una had her entire life ahead of her, and now she was free to live the way she wanted. She could have parties, could socialize and enjoy herself. I read between the lines of what Julia had offered so far, and it sounded like life hadn't been too fun until that point.

"There were a lot of men at the party." It was impossible to miss them. They crowded around Una like she was the queen bee.

Julia laughed fondly. "Yes, but she saw through them. All they wanted was her money, and they knew her parents' deaths meant she had control over it."

"But she was so beautiful, too. I can't believe none of them had a legitimate crush on her."

"Just the same. She trusted very few people." She said it with a sigh. "She tried very hard to be a different sort of person than her father was, and in many ways she succeeded. She was much more generous, giving. She enjoyed people, loved matching wits with anyone brave enough to attempt it. She wasn't as mistrusting and cynical in those days as Mr. Howell… Still, she had her funny little ways. Her apprehensions. And as she grew older, she grew more cynical."

"Is that why she never got married?"

Julia nodded. "Not for lack of interested parties, I can tell you that. I lost count of how many proposals she turned down. She used to say she didn't have time for marriage, that her life was already busy enough."

Becca surprised me by giggling, leaning forward to

look at me from across the album. "Who does that remind me of?"

"Oh, don't tell me that." Julia shook her head and clicked her tongue in disappointment. "Never fool yourself into believing you're too busy for love. My marriage didn't end well, but I'll never regret it. It was the reason I had my son, and my grandson."

I shot Becca a look to warn her away from asking about Julia's family. Her mouth snapped shut, telling me she'd been about to do just that.

Julia continued as she flipped the pages. "In the end, even Una realized she'd made a mistake. It was her biggest regret, never settling down. She had her independence, certainly, but it was cold comfort in her later years. Sure, she had plenty of friends, but it wasn't the same. I think that's why she ended up—"

"Excuse me." There was a knock on the open door before a woman in a pantsuit strode into the room. "Mrs. Lewis, I'd like to speak with these young ladies, if you wouldn't mind."

Well, that was that. I knew our good luck couldn't last forever. Becca shot me a panicked look, but what could we do? I turned to Julia and put my hand over hers, patting gently. "Thank you so much for taking the time to sit with us. It's been wonderful, talking with you."

Julia was obviously confused, laughing faintly at the situation. "It occurs to me we never got down to just why you came to see me today."

"I came in as a favor for someone who wanted to see how you were doing." It wasn't exactly a lie. There were lots of people who wanted to know how Julie was doing. Just nobody who actually cared about her, as a person. I couldn't shake the feeling of sadness as Becca said goodbye before the two of us joined the administrator out in the hall.

She didn't look angry, though, which felt like it could be a good sign. "I'm sorry, ladies, but we can't have strangers visiting our residents. I placed a call to Mrs. Lewis's caretaker, Lawrence Bradley, and he didn't recognize either of your names so I have no choice but to ask you to leave."

"I thought Mr. Bradley was Miss Howell's attorney."

"He oversees the Howell estate, including the will Miss Howell put in place. He sees himself as Mrs. Lewis's caretaker now, and we are under strict orders to report any unknown visitors. I'm sorry, but..."

"I'll take care of this."

The three of us turned at the sound of a male voice. A man who just had to be Una's lawyer strode smartly down the hall in a bespoke suit and freshly-shined shoes. He might as well have been wearing a sign.

"Mr. Bradley." The woman practically bowed and scraped at the sight of him. I wondered just how much this facility depended upon people like him who made sure the bills were paid and the lights stayed on.

"Thank you for calling me." He turned to Becca and me, and I didn't have to know him personally to recognize the look of disgust he wore. "Ladies, allow me to show you out."

So much for keeping a low profile.

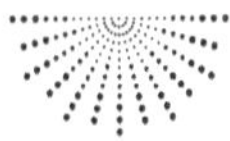

CHAPTER SIXTEEN

"Mr. Bradley, please, let me explain." We were outside, in the open courtyard between the lobby and the parking lot. At least he hadn't asked the guards to throw us out. "My friend and I only came to say hello to Mrs. Lewis. We weren't trying to upset anybody."

"Exactly how do you know her?" He raised an eyebrow, his dark eyes bouncing back and forth between the two of us. He looked to be in his mid-forties, tops, with just a touch of gray at his temples. Just like so many men, getting more attractive with time. It wasn't fair.

He wouldn't go for any vague answers, that much was clear. What was the point of maintaining the act? "You want the truth?"

"I would very much appreciate it."

Becca drew breath like she was ready to talk, but I nudged her gently before jumping in. "I was at the auction on Friday with a friend of mine who won the Reynolds desk. Being around all that history made me think about Miss Lewis. I heard she moved here from… was it her son's home or her grandson's? I can't remember which I heard."

He pursed his lips, eyes narrowing as they moved over me. "Exactly who are you?"

"I'm sorry. My name is Darcy Harmon. I own a bookstore in Cape Hope, and my mother owns a café next door. My entire life I've heard stories of the Howells and the other esteemed families in the area." I was making it up on the fly, but I didn't think I was doing a bad job of it. He seemed somewhat convinced, anyway. "In fact, I feel like I've seen you around before. Maybe you've stopped in for one of Mom's blueberry muffins."

He snapped his fingers. "Sure, that little coffee shop down the block from the beach? Sweet Nothings, right?"

Success. Now he at least knew I was from Cape Hope, and anybody with half an imagination would accept my gossip story. It boosted my confidence. "That's right! It's basically the crossroads of the entire town. I spent most of my time there as a kid, so I heard all of the news—even when Mom tried to keep it away from my innocent ears." We all laughed over that, even if Becca's laughter was a little too high-pitched to be natural. Good thing I was doing the talking.

"Come to think of it..." He stroked his chin. "I remember seeing you at the auction. Right, and your friend had that dramatic little bidding war, didn't he?"

"That would be him." We shared another laugh. "Honestly, we had no ill intentions here. It's just that, I don't know, I thought maybe she could use a visitor. I understand she's sort of on her own now, without her family."

"Yes, she's very lucky Ms. Howell provided as generously as she did. I'll leave it at that." He sounded pretty sour, though, which spoke volumes. "I'm sorry. You'll have to excuse me for being suspicious, but there's so many ghouls running around."

"Ghouls?" It was the first time Becca had said a word.

"Oh, you know." He rolled his eyes with a groan. "People who only want to know about Una. How she died. Where her money went. It's disgusting. They didn't know her, had never met her, yet they act like they're entitled to know about her personal life."

I didn't have to see Becca to know she was shriveling up inside at the way the lawyer described people who shared her hobby. "Mrs. Lewis is very lucky to have you. To keep them away, I mean."

"I would joke and say it's become a full-time job, but it wouldn't be far from the truth." Once again, disgust washed over his features. He looked over toward the building with a sigh. "It's what Una would've wanted. The two of them were like sisters. It meant a lot to her, knowing someone who meant so much wouldn't have to worry about money or a home for the rest of her life." There was so much genuine fondness in his voice.

"It was very sweet of her to care that much. A lot of people wouldn't care about their employees, no matter how long they worked." The more I heard about Una, the more I liked her.

"She was a special person. It took a while to get to know her, but once she accepted you into her inner circle? It meant something." He put a hand to his chest. The lines at the corners of his eyes softened. "And when somebody she knew needed help, the way she knew Julia would, you could bet she'd swoop in and take care of things."

"I guess that means you were part of the inner circle?" I grinned, playful, hoping to get as much information out of him as I could. And even as I did, I knew it made me no better than the people I'd been making snide comments about for days. I was a ghoul, the sort of person Lawrence wanted to keep away from Julia.

"A woman in Una's position found it difficult to trust many people. Over time, however, we developed a warm relationship. She was a fine, wonderful person. Which is why it sets my teeth on edge, knowing so many people have reduced her to nothing more than a name, a question mark."

"A question mark?" I exchanged a glance with Becca

"I thought you said you knew all the gossip." He narrowed his eyes, suspicious now, though he tried to hide it behind a bland smile.

"Oh, you mean her death," I hastened to answer, to which he nodded slowly. "That's very sad. I agree. Do you think that's why so many people came out for the auction?"

He scoffed, rolling his eyes. "I wouldn't be surprised. Though the bidding war your friend got into was easily the most exciting thing that happened."

I couldn't help but grin. "That was sort of exciting, wasn't it?"

"I could tell you thought so, throwing in a bid of

your own." He laughed when I blushed. "And how is your friend enjoying the desk?"

"He loves it." Out of the corner of my eye, I could see Becca giving me a confused look, but I ignored it.

"I have to admit, I never would've expected that sort of interest in a plain, old desk. Nobody else seemed to care very much."

"To each their own, right?" I shrugged, laughing. "Well, we've already taken too much of your time. And I'm sorry for any inconvenience we might have caused, making you come all this way from your office."

Then I patted my pockets, looking around on the ground. "Shoot. I think my phone fell out of my pocket. Would it be okay if I went in to grab it? Maybe it slid between the couch cushions."

He frowned for a split second but shrugged. "Go ahead."

I left him to chat with Becca, who looked completely bewildered. I could only hope she wouldn't say anything to give us away as I hurried back into the building, speeding past the front desk and down the hall before anyone could notice me. Meanwhile, my phone sat in my purse, just as it always had.

Something about the way he used Una's first name while using Julia's last name stuck out to me. It was enough to make me wonder just what sort of relationship they had—and whether he might be making more out of it now that she was gone and unable to deny it.

Julia looked up in surprise when I darted into the room. "I'm sorry, I don't mean to startle you." I looked over my shoulder before crouching in front of her chair, where she'd gone back to her crochet. "You were about to say something before that lady came in and interrupted us earlier."

She set her work in her lap, laughing softly. "I was? I'm sorry, my memory isn't what it used to be."

Not exactly the sort of thing that inspired confidence in a girl, but I pressed ahead. "You were saying something about Una being alone. And how that was why she ended up doing something. But you didn't get the chance to say what that something was."

"Oh." She scowled. "I was about to say, she ended up getting involved with that younger man. Far too young for her, but she never did want to listen to reason once she made her mind up."

"And who was that young man?" Though I already had a pretty good idea.

"Her lawyer. Lawrence Bradley."

I patted her hand before standing. "Thank you." I then fished my phone out of the purse on my way from her room, making sure to hold it in my hand so it was visible when I joined Becca and Lawrence out front.

Once we were in the car and on our way home, Becca let out a huge sigh. "Remind me never to do that again."

"Never to do what again?" Meanwhile, my palms were still sweaty. I rubbed them on my thighs and tried to ignore how my hands shook.

"I don't know how you and your sister ever made a habit of slinking around. I was sure that lawyer was going to call the cops on us."

I almost shouted out a laugh. Adrenaline was still coursing through my veins. "And I thought you were the confident one."

"I couldn't have known he would show up. You know who he is, right?"

"I would guess he's the executor of Una's will and the person who manages her estate. And he was her boyfriend."

Becca gasped—though not for the reason I expected. "How did you know that?"

Whoa! "Wait. Did you know that?"

She gave me a sideways glance. "Of course I did! Everybody knows that."

"You could've told me! That's the whole reason I went

back inside. I wanted to ask Julia what she was about to say before we were interrupted. She was trying to say it was Una's loneliness that drove her toward Lawrence."

"Sorry. There's so many different things about the case that I can't keep track of it all at once. If I knew we'd end up seeing him, I might've filled you in."

She had a point. We couldn't have known he would end up on the scene. My hands were finally not shaking as much. "What kind of a feeling did you get from him?"

"He seems like a nice guy. He's definitely made sure Julia is taken care of. That says a lot about him."

"I was thinking the same thing. He could've been sneaky about it and put her in some dump so he could get the money for himself." I tapped my fingers on my lap, mulling it over as Becca drove. Normally, I would've been annoyed at being the passenger—my car was still out of commission, and I hadn't yet got around to arranging for a new one—but at least I could stare off into the distance and think. "Then again, she does have family. They might be looking over his shoulder."

She scoffed. "Trust me. They aren't."

Her confidence surprised me. "What do you mean? Do they not care?"

"Her son passed away last year. And her grandson is in prison."

"Get out!"

"Can you guess why he's there?" She didn't give me a chance to think about it before blurting it out. "He was stealing things from Una's house and selling them."

"You're kidding me. Why didn't you mention that before?"

"I didn't know before today." She gave me a coy little smile before turning back toward the road ahead. "He told me about it when you were inside. The kid's name is Michael and he had a drug problem. He was selling off whatever he could steal."

The plot thickened. "What are the odds, do you think, that he knew Una would provide for his grandmother in her will?"

"Believe me, I'm way ahead of you and was already wondering that."

"Great minds think alike." It made sense. Somebody who'd already been caught stealing from her seemed like a natural suspect, even if there was a big difference between theft and murder. "Of course, the police didn't pursue him, since they were so fast to rule it an accident."

"There wasn't much police involvement. That was

a real risk you took, saying your dad worked on the case. But then I guess somebody working at the nursing home wouldn't have known about that."

"What you mean, the police weren't involved?" This was the first I was hearing about it.

"There was a private investigation. But that was it. You didn't know that, either?" When all I could do was gape at her, she shook her head, still focused on the road. "I'm actually kind of disappointed in you."

"Ew."

That made her laugh. "I'm just saying, you're usually all over this sort of thing, but it seems like you haven't done much research on your own."

"Because I keep trying to avoid the whole thing! I never wanted to do this in the first place, going and visiting the poor old woman."

"No, but you sure as heck came up with a reason to score another minute alone with her, didn't you?" She giggled at the way I sputtered. "So now that you've met her, and the lawyer who was Una's boyfriend toward the end of her life, are you still determined to walk away from this?"

"You already know the answer."

She snickered. "Yes, I do."

"You know, you sound a lot like my sister when you get smug." Then, because she snickered again, I turned the tables. "Are you going to tell Max about this?"

Her cheeks flushed. "No comment." Of course, that meant I had to tease her the entire rest of the way back to the store. Just because the man had a talent for making my skin crawl didn't mean she wasn't allowed to like him.

Even if I was starting to seriously question her judgment.

I should've known from the way my sister froze in panic when we walked into the store that something was up. I considered backing out and pretending I never came in but it was too late for that. "What's wrong?"

She slid a folded piece of paper across the front counter. "I tried. I really did. But he insisted."

"Who insisted?" I unfolded the paper as I asked the question, and the note scrawled across it provided the answer.

Meet me on the boardwalk at six so we can talk about your road trip this morning. And it was signed by none other than Pete.

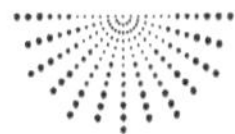

CHAPTER SEVENTEEN

There was no way out of it. At six o'clock, I made sure to be on the boardwalk. My feet were like a lead, making me fight for every step. Who could blame me? I knew exactly what I was in for, thanks to my sister's inability to tell a white lie when it had to do with anybody other than herself.

"What was I supposed to do? He saw right through me. He made a crack about how easy it is to read my face, and how it must run in the family." Yes, that definitely sounded like something Pete would say. When it had been clear Emma was on the verge of tears thanks to hormones and the fact that she knew she had let me down, there had been no choice but to let her off the hook. It wasn't her fault, anyway. She was only trying to help.

Pete was waiting for me near the stairs leading up from the sidewalk. He had his back to me, his gaze moving over the people walking past on the boardwalk. There weren't as many people as there would be at the height of the season, but there were still a good number of visitors who didn't want to let go of summer. If I wasn't so full of dread, I might've enjoyed the sight of his broad back and shoulders, the way the late day sunlight brought out the touches of red in his hair.

I was a big girl. I could handle this. At least, I hoped so.

I forced myself up the steps, wearing a smile I didn't feel and tugging his sleeve when I reached him. "Hello. Thanks for the note."

He continued surveying the boardwalk. "Is there anything you want to tell me?" The man was skilled at keeping his tone light, no matter what was running under the surface.

"You should wear yellow more often. It makes your skin glow." When his eyes shifted my way, narrowing, I held up both hands in surrender. "Okay. You already know what I did today, so can we skip ahead past the part where you scold me like I'm a naughty kid?"

His mouth twitched but he managed to suppress

any good humor. "Fine. Consider yourself scolded. Why can't you let this go?"

"Now, hang on a second. This, I did as a favor to Becca, and nothing else. It was Emma who put the idea in her head in the first place."

"If I didn't know how Emma could be thanks to the things Joe says about her, I might not believe you."

My jaw jutted out. "What does Joe say about her?" And did I have to warn him not to talk smack about my sister?

"Easy. It's just storytelling, not complaining." His expression softened a little. "You're very protective of her."

"I'm protective of everybody. Sue me." We started walking, taking our time. There was a nice breeze coming off the water, and it lifted my hair from the back of my neck. I took a few deep breaths, telling myself to release the stress that had built up throughout the day as I watched the clock, waiting for my execution. Now it looked like that execution had been postponed at least for a little while.

"I just hope you didn't terrorize that poor old woman."

"Not even a little bit. She had us sit with her and go through her photo album, actually." When Pete shot me a dark look, indignation bubbled up in my chest. "It was her idea, thank you very much. And it made her very happy. She said nobody ever looks at her pictures. I got the feeling she's pretty lonely."

"I guess she must be. I don't think there are many people left in her life besides whatever friends she might have made there."

I gave him a playful nudge. "So you know about her?"

He muttered something unintelligible, but it didn't sound complimentary. "You are enough to drive a saint to swear, you know that?"

"Uh, thank you?"

He burst out laughing, which came as a relief. "Yes, I know about her. I looked her up. I wouldn't have if it wasn't for your sister dropping her name."

"Do you know about her grandson being in prison?"

"I do." There was a hint of suspicion to his voice, but I chose to ignore it. "I also know Michael Lewis, Jr. was released three months ago."

I was ready to burst out of my skin. "You're kidding!"

"No, I'm not. But I don't see what that has to do with anything."

"Well, he's out of prison now. He's been free to come and go. And oh, surprise, there was a big auction of Una's possessions. Is it such a stretch that he'd want to get his hands on her diary, in case she had written something about him being a thief?"

"We already know he's a thief, though, so that wouldn't prove anything new."

"What if she knew about other things he took that he hasn't yet been prosecuted for?"

"Darcy, I just don't know."

I couldn't help but growl. It seemed so obvious to me, and so obvious he was being deliberately obtuse. "Don't you at least think it's interesting? Somebody we know stole items from the house and sold them because he needed to get his hands on money. Then, Una just happened to accidentally fall down the stairs when there was nobody else at home? What if Michael knew his grandmother wouldn't be there, and Una would be all alone? Wasn't Julia supposed to be visiting family when Una fell?"

"How do you know that?" He came to a stop, turning to me. "I didn't find anything about that in our files. Then again, there isn't much on the case."

"That's because there was a private investigator involved. They didn't want the police getting into it."

He raked his fingers through his hair. "Who is they?"

"How should I know? Probably her lawyer. I guess he would be the person overseeing all that stuff."

He stared over my shoulder, out toward the water. "Well, sometimes it's like that with wealthy families. They want to keep things on the down-low, to keep them quiet so people don't talk."

"But Una didn't have any family left. She was the last of the Howells, wasn't she?"

He shrugged. "Well, then I guess the lawyer was the person calling the shots."

"But it does seem like he wanted to protect her, somehow. After all, they were so close." I watched Pete's face when I said this.

A shadow moved across his countenance. "So you know about that, too."

I resisted the urge to groan. "Let me guess. There was something about it in the file."

"No, smarty." He ran a hand over the back of his neck, which I recognized instantly as something he did when he was feeling put on the spot. "I did a little research in other places."

"You trolled the message boards?" I couldn't help but giggle.

"Well? Why not? It's clear you have no intention of

disassociating yourself from this situation. I figured I might as well learn everything I could."

I raised a brow. "Now, you can't tell me the whole thing doesn't seem suspicious."

We started off again, sidestepping the group of kids running around with ice cream cones in hand. It made me think about the time I did the same thing with my sister, then ended up dropping my cone. She shared hers with me. The only time she'd ever shared a dessert.

"Of course, it seems suspicious. That doesn't mean you need to get involved."

"Trust me. I don't want to be involved, but it's too late for that. Now, the lawyer knows me. I've met Julia. I've even met with Brian Mills—"

"Who?"

Darn it. "He's an author… who may or may not have been the other person interested in the desk." I braced myself for what I knew was coming.

Only it didn't come. "At least you're being honest."

"What? You're not going to give me the third degree? No threatening to tell my daddy on me?"

He narrowed his eyes. "That does sound tempting. Don't worry. Ethan has been keeping me on top of the situation. Unlike you, he believes in going to the police with information like this. And he told me you went with them, because it was either that or let Max go by himself."

Why did I find myself angry with Ethan? It was the right thing to do. Wasn't it?

"You're annoyed." Pete snickered when I looked his way, ready to deny it. "Don't even bother. It's all over your face."

"I guess I don't much like the idea of somebody going behind my back and telling stories about me."

"That's not the way it was."

"Even so. That's how it feels."

"Unlike you, Darcy Harmon, some people in this town have a little bit of faith in the police. And considering his was the home that was broken into, why wouldn't he be the one to come to us?"

"Okay, okay. I get it."

We walked in companionable silence for a while, and it occurred to me not for the first time how much I missed his presence. I glanced his way from the corner of my eye and wondered if it would be weird for me to ask about his personal life.

Only one way to find out. "How have you been?"

"Pretty good. You?" We both laughed at that, since he pretty much knew.

"It's just that you've been kind of a closed book lately. Anything new going on?"

"Why don't you ask me what I know you want to ask?"

"Oh, please, tell me what you think is on my mind. You know how it thrills me when you act like a mind reader."

He barked out a laugh. "You want to know if I'm still seeing the woman I was dating a while back."

"Boy, you don't have an ego problem at all."

"Don't even pretend. This has nothing to do with ego. It's just that I don't see any reason why we can't be upfront with each other."

He had a point. "Okay. Yes, I was wondering."

"Well, I'm not seeing her anymore. Nor am I seeing anyone else. Satisfied?"

"Oh, definitely. I'll sleep so much better tonight."

We headed over to one of the handful of pizza stalls still in business through the end of the month and ordered a couple of slices which we ate on our way back to where we started. At least when we were chewing, there was only so much conversation we could have.

It was still fully light out by the time we were ready to part ways on Main Street. My heart sank a little and I wished it wouldn't. Why couldn't I have appreciated Pete this much when there was still a chance for us? Now, I had no idea where I stood. It would be better to think of us as friends and nothing more.

"You okay getting home?" I couldn't tell whether he wanted me to say yes or no, whether he wanted the excuse to walk me home or not. I decided honesty was the best policy.

"I'm sure I'll be fine, but thanks for asking. I'll see you later, okay?"

He looked slightly skeptical but jerked his chin in response, anyway, before turning and heading home. I watched him go for a few seconds before realizing it probably looked like I was staring at his backside. Which I may or may not have been doing.

I was halfway home when my phone rang. It seemed like everybody wanted a piece of my time, but then that was normally the case, anyway. This time, it was Ethan. "Don't tell me you're going to read me the riot act, now, too."

He waited a beat. "And hello to you as well."

"Sorry. It's been one of those days."

"Well, for what it's worth, I have no intention of getting on your case. I was actually calling to see if you're free Wednesday night."

I went warm all of a sudden, and my pulse picked up speed. I'd been waiting for this. And now, I didn't know what to do. "I'm sure I could free up some time, either way."

"Wow, that sounds flattering."

He would be a sarcastic jerk about it, wouldn't he? "What are you asking, Ethan?"

"I'm asking if you have time to come to dinner with me. I've kept you waiting long enough, not that I meant to keep you waiting. It wasn't a conscious choice. Can we go back to before I started talking?"

There was something charming about listening to him scramble around for the right thing to say. He was normally so sure of himself, confident. I couldn't help feeling a little flattered, like I was the reason for it.

Rather than torture him, I agreed. "Okay. Let's pretend we're just getting on the phone this very second. Hi, Ethan. Thanks for calling. What's up?"

"You are the worst sometimes."

"Is that supposed to make me want to go out with you?" I couldn't help but laugh when he groaned. "Fine. I mean, yes. I would like to go to dinner with you. Thank you for finally getting around to asking for real."

He offered to pick me up at six for dinner "out of town," though he didn't say exactly where we'd be heading. I decided to leave it up to him.

Besides, I now had more than enough on my mind.

Such as what to wear on a first date with somebody whom I couldn't decide whether to kiss or kill. When I reached the house, I bounded up the stairs to my apartment. There was music coming from Poppy's, telling me she was home.

I banged on the door. "There's a fashion emergency and I need your help!"

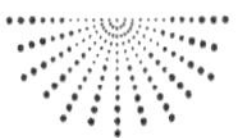

CHAPTER EIGHTEEN

It was amazing, really, what the idea of going on an actual date did to my mind. My confidence. If I was only going over to Ethan's kitchen to hang out and give him trouble, I wouldn't think twice about what I was wearing or how I smelled. Okay, maybe I would care about how I smelled, but I wouldn't check to make sure I put on deodorant five or six times before coming face-to-face with him.

Just breathe, girl. I did my best while waiting on the porch, willing myself to stop fidgeting, to stop pacing. After a great deal of deliberation, Poppy had decided I would look best in a simple dress and sweater, flat shoes, a little bit of makeup. "You don't want to make it look like you're trying too hard. But you still look gorgeous." I wasn't so sure about gorgeous, but at least

I managed to clean up well. It was a far cry from my usual uniform of jeans and whatever shirt my hand happened to land on as I was getting dressed.

I recognized Ethan's car pulling down the street. My heart immediately leaped up into my throat and I decided I hated everything about my outfit. And my hair! Whose big idea was it to leave my hair down? Too late now. He had already seen me, was already pulling to a stop. I was about to start down the steps when he rolled down his window. "Wait right there."

Just like him to throw me a curveball right off the bat. I waited, my stomach in knots, my hands sweating. Would he notice if I checked one more time to make sure I didn't stink?

When he stepped out of the car, I was glad there was some distance between us. He didn't hear me gasp at the sight of him in a suit. An actual suit. It was the first time I had seen him out of work or casual clothes. It was gray, well-fitted, and naturally he wore a black shirt underneath. I was starting to think it was his favorite color. While he usually didn't adhere to the whole "shaving every day" thing, his cheeks were smooth, and his hair was shorter than it had been just a few days earlier.

Best part of all? He was carrying flowers. "For you."

He handed them to me when he reached the bottom of the stairs. "I wanted to do this right."

I could hardly believe my eyes. "They're beautiful."

"Olivia put them together special for you." Yes, and I sincerely hoped she hadn't charged what I knew a bouquet like this was worth. I had picked up a few things while filling in for her at the florist shop.

Then again, what would've been the harm in letting a man spend a little money on me? I buried my nose in the roses, hydrangeas, and daisies. "Thank you so much. Let me run up and put them in water. I'll be right out." He waited while I dashed up the stairs.

Poppy flung her door open when she heard me at my door. "What's wrong?" Then, she noticed the flowers, the sight of which made her touch the back of her hand to her forehead. "I think I might faint."

"Hush."

"Here. I'll take care of them for you. Get back out there." She took the flowers and cradled them in her arms like they were some precious thing. "How does he look?"

"Honestly?" I fanned myself. "I didn't expect this. This is a whole other level sort of thing."

"Enjoy yourself, for heaven's sake. Stop over-thinking everything." She stopped short of pushing me down the stairs, but just barely. I went down on trembling legs and hoped I wouldn't make a fool of myself.

Gosh, he looked good. Extremely dashing. Downright hot, even. My heart did a little flutter when he reached for my hand. "Come on. We have a reservation. I think you're going to like it."

"Where are we going?"

"I would try to be mysterious, but what's the point? We have a reservation at the Riviera, in Paradise city."

"I know the executive chef! Robbie Klein. He's great. He worked at the café for a summer."

"I know. He told me so. We run in the same circles."

"What a small world." At least I knew we were in for a terrific night, though something told me I would've enjoyed being with Ethan no matter where we went. He was like a new person, charming and thoughtful and oh, so handsome. I only hoped my heart could take it.

"I only have one rule tonight." He opened the passenger side door, meeting my gaze with a grin before stepping aside so I could slide in. "Let's not talk about my cousin or Una Howell or any of it."

"Music to my ears." We were both laughing as I climbed in, and he joined me a moment later before pulling down the street and heading for the parkway.

Funny thing, though. If we couldn't talk about Max

or Una now, there was only one thing left—work. I didn't mind that, though. He understood what it was like to put everything he had into his business, his dream. As he told me about his day, it occurred to me that knowing he could relate was one of the things I liked best about him. I didn't have to explain what went into running a business, building it from scratch, trying to find new ways of bringing in customers.

I didn't have to feel bad for liking it the way I did, either. There was no need to apologize, no need to feel like there was something wrong with me because I was so heavily involved in my work.

The drive to the hotel passed in the blink of an eye. If I hadn't been so hungry, I might've wished we'd gotten stuck in traffic. Then again, even a couple of years after opening, Robbie's restaurant was just as popular as ever. If we had missed our reservation, something told me we wouldn't have been able to get another one easily. Even if we both knew the executive chef.

The executive chef who came out to say hello after we'd been seated. "I told them to let me know when you arrived." Robbie kissed my cheek before shaking Ethan's hand. "It's a small world, isn't it? I didn't know the two of you were—"

Ethan cleared his throat. "Yeah, Darcy was

commenting on the size of the world when I told her we knew each other." So he didn't want Robbie to assume we were dating. That was fine, especially since the devilish part of me got a kick out of seeing him flustered on my account.

Now I understood why we got the best table in the house, the one closest to the beach. We had a perfect view of the ocean, sparkling in the evening light. The whole thing was pretty romantic on the whole, and I couldn't help but feel more flattered than ever knowing how much thought Ethan had put into this.

When we were alone again, I had to comment. "In case I forget to say it later, thank you for this. It means a lot."

"I kept you waiting long enough, so I figured I'd better do it right." His dark eyes sparkled in the light from the candle sitting between us on the table. When he smiled, I didn't know what to do with myself. It was like I forgot how to breathe.

Oh, no. I wasn't falling in love with him, was I?

Good thing our food came quickly, or else I might have done something embarrassing like try to kiss him. "Chef Robert created a special tasting menu just for the two of you." Our server was all smiles as she slid the first course in front of us. An assortment of amuse-bouche to whet our appetites. I just about fell over and died when I tasted the guanciale, and the shot glasses of gazpacho had me wanting to lick up every last drop. I had to remind myself to behave.

Everything was perfection. Delicate pan-seared duck, a baby lamb chop over mashed potatoes I would seriously have killed for an entire bowl of. "The man has come a long way since Cape Hope." I scraped what was left of the potatoes off my plate and wondered if it would be rude to ask for the recipe. Or for seconds, at least.

"I'm telling you, whenever I feel like I'm doing pretty well for myself, I visit Robbie's restaurant and remember I'm practically an amateur."

"You are not an amateur. Don't even play games like that." I held my knife up, pretending to threaten him with it. "Unless you're fishing for compliments."

"You know I don't do that."

"True. You're usually too busy bragging about yourself to pretend to be modest."

He grimaced. "I take a woman out to a nice dinner, and she's still snarky."

I couldn't help but laugh, a little sheepish. "You're right. I'm sorry. It's so easy to fall into old habits."

I got a begrudging smile in return. "Don't be too sorry. It's part of the reason why I like you."

"Be careful, or else you'll never hear the end of it."

Our pasta course came out next, a gorgeous fettuccine carbonara that I just about devoured in one bite. I told myself I should savor the food, especially since I was not alone and was in fact surrounded by people. But it was just too delicious.

When I found Ethan frowning, however, I rethought my strategy. "Sorry. I need to control myself."

"Who? Oh, no, sorry. Believe me, I want to shovel everything into my mouth at once."

"What's wrong, then?"

He groaned, reaching into his jacket pocket. "I'm sorry. My phone's been buzzing almost nonstop since the second course. I've been ignoring it, but I keep getting calls."

"By all means, see who it is."

"That's the problem. I know who it is." And when he checked, he only rolled his eyes. "Just as I guessed."

"Is it somebody we promised not to talk about tonight?"

"No wonder you're so good at solving mysteries." At least he managed a tiny smile. "He's called six times."

I bit my lip, looking from him to the phone and back again. "Has he left voicemails?"

"Indeed, he has."

"It might be serious. Maybe you should check, at least."

"And maybe he gets sweaty and shaky the second nobody's paying attention to him." When I only tipped my head to the side, disapproving, he doubled down. "No. Tonight was supposed to be about us. Not about him."

The fact that he referred to us as *us* made the back of my neck tingle. I shrugged it off, chalked it up to family issues not being my business, and decided to let it go. I could lead a horse to water but I couldn't make him check his voicemail.

After we finished, the final course being a homemade waffle topped with butter semifreddo, Robbie came out again to ask how we liked it.

There was only one appropriate response as far as I was concerned. "Would it be wrong if I asked you to marry me?"

"Darn it, you're too late." Yes, I had forgotten Robbie was remarried. I had to give him credit. If my spouse had framed me for murder, it would've taken a lot longer than a couple of years to find somebody new. It might've been enough to make me give up on relationships altogether. Only thanks to my sister was he a free man, while his ex-wife rotted in prison the way she deserved.

We left with promises to come back soon, then walked slowly to the car. "I think I gained ten pounds." Ethan patted his stomach with a groan, "Maybe I should've been a little smarter about weighing myself down with all that food."

"Oh? Why? What else did you have in mind?" I knew how my question sounded and, frankly, that was how I wanted it to sound. It was pretty bold of me, flirting like that, but I couldn't help it. Everything about the night had been so perfect. Like something out of a dream. There were times I almost wanted to pinch myself in case I really was dreaming and the charming, absolutely gorgeous man with me was a figment of my imagination.

Then again, pinching myself would have broken the spell, and I didn't want to risk that, either.

We stopped at the car, and I turned to him, still grinning. Only he wasn't grinning. He looked deeply serious as he came closer, leaving barely enough room for a breeze to pass between us.

"For starters?" He then took my face in his hands and I let him, tipping my head back so our mouths could line up as he leaned in.

My eyes closed.

He grunted.

My eyes opened. He was wearing an expression I knew all too well.

"I'm sorry. He's calling me again." Sure enough, I could hear the buzzing without so many voices filling the air around us.

I sighed, a little deflated. "You really should see what he wants. He's not going to stop."

"I swear, he's lucky I'm not keeping a running list of everything he owes me." He pulled out his phone and swiped almost viciously across the screen. "This had better be good."

Suddenly his head snapped up, his eyes widening. "Brian called Max. Somebody tried to run him down two nights ago and he was just released from the hospital today."

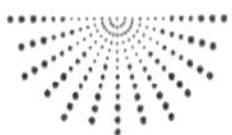

CHAPTER NINETEEN

"I only wish I could've gotten a look at the guy." Brian's voice came out from the speaker in Ethan's car, where we sat in the parking lot. He hadn't even started driving us home, mostly because I had insisted he get Brian's number from his cousin so he could call him right away.

"You got very lucky." I exchanged a look with Ethan. "He might not have stopped if it hadn't been for the other car coming by."

"I'm telling you. Here I am, thinking I'll try to get healthy and go for a run, and this is what happens. I was safer when I was a slob." At least he had a sense of humor.

I wasn't sure I could've been so cheerful in his position, after receiving fifteen stitches to the scalp and breaking my left femur. "So, you were out for a run. The car sideswiped you."

"Right. They came at me from behind—rather, I should say he came at me from behind."

"I thought you said you didn't get a look at them, though."

"I guess there was blood in my eyes."

I cringed, squeezing my own eyes shut.

"Sorry. I don't mean to snap at you," Brian added.

"It's okay."

Ethan patted my arm. "And then he stopped the car and got out?"

"Yes, for sure. I assumed they were getting out to help me. Like it was all an accident. Except he picked up a rock and started walking my way with it in his hand, hanging down by his leg."

"Oh, my God." I covered my face with my hands. It was too much to imagine.

"I knew then that I was in trouble, but my leg was broken. I couldn't get up. I could only call out for help, but it was just the two of us until headlights showed up down the road, heading in our direction."

"And then he ran?"

"He ran. He dropped the rock, took off running for the car, and flew out of there. Luckily I was able to flag down the car that approached, and they called for an ambulance. I only wish I had gotten a look at the guy or the car."

"You were sort of busy worrying about what would happen next. I don't think anybody could blame you for that." It was tough to imagine, being so helpless. Seeing somebody coming at him with a rock in their hand when they realized they hadn't finished the job. Who would do such a thing?

In my mind, the answer was obvious.

"Now I know your cousin wasn't lying when he said somebody was following him around. I thought for a minute he might've been making it up just to make himself out to be the victim. I actually had to apologize to him. Can you imagine?" Brian laughed. "It's not really funny, but these painkillers are a miracle."

Ethan rolled his eyes. "I hope you lay low for a while."

"I plan to. I'm having my sister and her kids out for a little while, so I won't be here alone. She insisted. Older sisters can be like that."

"I can relate—though I'm the older sister." When Max wasn't around, Brian was actually nice to talk to. He seemed like a decent person. That made it even harder to come to grips with what had almost happened to him.

"I have to ask," Ethan said as he shot me an apprehensive look. "Has this sort of thing ever happened to you before? I mean, do you have…"

"Enemies? None that I'm aware of. I know your cousin wants to make it sound like there's a lot of drama surrounding our lives, but trust me, that's not normally the case. The most that usually ever happens is getting snitch-tagged in a bad review online. Of course, there's sometimes a little bit of backbiting, but nothing serious."

Now, I had to ask. "Do you think this has anything to do with, you know, Una?"

"I can't imagine how it would. But I'm starting to wonder. First there's a car following Max around, then I get run down. It would seem like the auction is what ties us together. I can't imagine anybody being able to link us, though. He wasn't there."

I snapped my fingers when it came to me. "Pete told me Julia Lewis's grandson has been out of prison for a few months now. I wonder if he was at the auction. I certainly wouldn't have known who to look for."

Brian gasped. "The grandson? He's out?"

"Looks that way." I noticed Ethan was staring at me and realized too late it might've been because I'd mentioned Pete's name. "He was giving me grief about getting involved." His expression was unreadable.

"I haven't seen an updated picture of him in a while. I might've walked right past him at the auction and never knew it. That could be it. He could be the connection."

Ethan shook his head. "No offense, but that still doesn't make any sense. You didn't win the desk. There was no way for Julia's grandson to know anything about you. There was no reason for him to feel threatened by you."

"If he knew the diary was in the desk and saw the two of us going back and forth over it, he might've put two and two together and figured I was a threat, as well. Especially if, when he got his hands on the diary and read its contents, he found evidence in there against him. He would be that much more determined to get anybody who suspected him out of the way."

"And you do suspect him?" Ethan prodded.

"I always have. He's always been the most logical guess." He chuckled. "You know, it's funny. As an author, I do my best not to rely on the most obvious answer. In this case, there's very few options. He rises to the top of the list no matter which angle I've tried to approach from."

I found myself needing to convince Ethan, who

still didn't look swayed. "It makes sense. We already know he was desperate for money. Una probably didn't make a secret of how she'd provided for Julia. He probably figured he could get her out of the way quickly, then take advantage of the money his grandmother would get from the will."

"I'm telling you. If those cops around there know what they're doing, they'll find him. I'm sure he's the missing piece." Then he seemed to think of something else. "And breaking into your house would be child's play for him, Ethan. He could've learned all kinds of tricks in the year-and-a-half he was in prison."

There was obvious excitement in Brian's voice, growing with every word.

Ethan jumped in before I could make things any worse. "Maybe you'd better take it easy. Get some rest. I'm sure all this excitement isn't going to help your head feel any better."

"You're right about that. I can only take so many of these pills at once." Then, Brian added one final sentiment in a serious voice. "Be careful."

It was just the two of us again once Ethan ended the call. We sat in silence for a moment, staring out the windshield. He spoke first. "So much for a nice evening."

"It was nice, though. Really nice." I found his hand

and laced my fingers through his. "You were doing really well there, Crosby."

"Thanks, Harmon." I could tell he felt flattered, though, grinning in spite of himself as he started the engine. I did wish Max had slightly better timing, since the build-up to that kiss was epic. We would have another chance, though. We had to.

It was getting dark, the sun now sinking below the horizon. He turned on the radio and found an oldies station which, unfortunately, was playing a song that had been popular when I was a little kid. "Oh, now I'm really going to lose my dinner."

"What are they thinking? That's not an oldie! I was in grade school when that came out!"

"I know!" Then I gave it some thought. "But you know, when my mom listened to oldies when I was a kid, they were playing songs that were probably twenty years old or so."

"Stop that. I don't want to listen to reason right now."

We both laughed, and I couldn't have been gladder. There was nothing like sitting in uncomfortable silence, neither of us wanting to talk about what happened to Brian—and what might've happened if he hadn't gotten lucky.

What did it take for somebody to pick up a rock on

their way to a man they had deliberately sideswiped? What was the man intending to do with that rock? I didn't have to think long or hard about that one. It was enough to make my blood run cold.

We both winced when a pair of high beams hit us from behind. "Come on! How rude can you be?" Ethan turned his head slightly away from the rearview mirror, where the lights reflected blindingly. He changed lanes, I assumed in hopes of the car passing us.

Only it didn't. The car changed lanes, too, the lights burning bright.

"What are they doing?" I turned in the seat, holding my hand in front of my eyes in hopes of blocking the glare. It was no use. I couldn't even see the kind of car it was, much less who was behind the wheel.

Maybe it was the conversation with Brian. Maybe it was all the food I had unceremoniously dumped down my throat. But all of a sudden, I didn't feel so well. "Ethan?"

"I know." It was barely a grunt, his teeth gritted. "Face forward. Make sure your belt is secure."

"Should I call the police?"

"Give it a minute." He gunned it, the car now flying down the mercifully quiet parkway. The few cars we encountered may as well have been standing still.

And sure enough, the car behind us picked up speed until it was practically on the bumper.

"What can we do?" My fingers dug into the upholstery and my right foot pressed against the floorboards like I could control the gas pedal that way.

"Aside from letting him run us off the road?"

"Yes, aside from that." I made the mistake of glancing at the speedometer and found we were going over eighty miles an hour and were creeping up on ninety.

"Call the police. Tell them what's happening, give them the next mile marker." Ethan zipped in and out of a cluster of cars and I squealed as I lost a couple of years from my life. "Sorry. Hurry up."

My hands were shaking too hard at first, but I forced myself to calm them enough to find my phone and make the call, turning on the speaker so Ethan could hear the dispatcher.

"We're traveling southbound on the Garden State Parkway and there's a car following us very closely with its high beams on. We can't seem to lose it." Because sure enough, no matter what Ethan did, that driver was right on top of us. I gave the dispatcher the mile marker as we passed. "We're going very fast." There were tears in my voice, I realized, which went with the tears threatening to spill over onto my cheeks.

The dispatcher's warm, encouraging voice filtered from the speaker. "There's a trooper about a mile up the road. I'll let them know to expect you."

I was about to thank her when suddenly, there was the sense of being shoved. I realized the driver had tapped the bumper on the driver's side, causing Ethan to swerve almost violently.

I screamed—I couldn't help it—while the dispatcher shouted. "What happened?"

"They're trying to run us off the road!" Thank goodness there hadn't been any cars around us, or else we would've slid right into them. The sight of flashing lights up ahead was the sweetest thing I'd ever seen.

"The trooper sees you coming. Pull over into the far right lane." Ethan did so while I covered my face with my shaking hands, weeping as softly as I could. That was the second time I'd seen my life flash before my eyes and I was getting sick and tired of it.

As soon as we stopped, Ethan reached for me. "I'm sorry. I'm sorry." He held me close. I felt his heart hammering away against my chest. Or maybe that was my heart.

"It's not your fault." Though I couldn't stop shaking, not even when the trooper knocked on the window. Ethan touched the button to roll it down.

The trooper leaned in. "Are you two all right?"

"Did you see the car? Did you even think to follow him?" Sure enough, the car had sped right past us, flying off into the night. The trooper had been too concerned with us.

"It's okay." The last thing we needed was for Ethan to get arrested for smarting off to a state trooper. "We're safe. That's what matters."

He turned back to me, brushing hair away from my forehead, his eyes darting over my face like he was making sure I was okay. "This time. What, are we supposed to lock ourselves up at home until this is all settled?"

The very thought was infuriating. That fury spread through me like a white-hot flame just as intense as the terror I'd only just suffered. "No. We're not going to do that. We're going to get to the bottom of this ourselves."

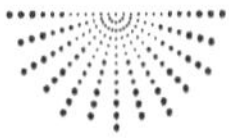

CHAPTER TWENTY

"Absolutely not. I won't allow this." Dad stood firm, shaking his head at my suggestion. "I can't believe you would suggest it."

"She'll be perfectly safe." Trixie placed a hand on my shoulder.

That earned her a patented George Harmon scowl. "With all due respect, Trixie, you have no way of knowing that."

"If you think the boys down at the station can't keep her safe, maybe that's the problem you need to be worried about right now." Trixie wasn't about to stand down, no matter how menacing he tried to be. She had known him for too long.

Besides, this could end up being a big story for her.

I wasn't naïve. I knew there was more than a little bit of self-interest in the way she defended me.

Dad's face started turning red. Good thing Joe jumped in when he did. "Honestly, it's not a terrible idea."

"You, too?" Dad threw his hands into the air. "Honestly, it's like the entire world is losing its mind and I'm the only sane person left."

"I know you're worried for her. The fact is, if we're going to find out who's behind this, we're going to have to draw them out." Joe held firm in the face of Dad's exasperation. "You know as well as I do we have very little to go on. Whoever this guy is, he's smart enough to cover his tracks."

"An experienced criminal would know how to do that, wouldn't he?" I looked around. "I mean, short of having Julia reach out to her grandson for a visit, we don't have any other way of trapping him."

Dad's eyes lit up. "Fine, then. Let the woman call this Michael person. Let him go visit her. Why do you have to be involved?"

"Dad. Come on. We can't put a nice lady in a situation like that. It would be cruel."

Ethan raised his hand. "Can I say something?"

Dad's head snapped around, his eyes blazing when

they found Ethan standing by my side door. "It depends."

Ethan cleared his throat, and under any other circumstance it might've thrilled me a little to see him look so nervous. But I knew how it felt when Dad was good and angry, when the full weight of his sizable temper turned my way, so my glee was more like sympathy. "The last thing I want is to see Darcy in a dangerous situation. But as long as this guy is out there, any situation could wind up being dangerous."

Yes, like coming back from a date. "This has to come to an end, Dad. Not just for me or for Ethan, but for Brian and Max, too. For anybody else Michael Lewis sees as a threat. If he killed Una and ran Brian down and chased us down the road, what else do you think he's capable of?"

"Why does it have to be you?" Dad's brows drew together, and I saw the pain in his expression. That was what sat at the core of this. Pain. Fear.

"Because I'm one of the people who was at the auction. He doesn't know I have nothing to do with any of this, that the desk was never meant for me. So either Trixie can put a story in the paper about how I have no clue, or she can write something that makes it look like I do have a clue."

Max shrugged, leaning in the doorway to the kitchen. "I think this is a good idea."

"I don't remember asking what you think about any of this."

All right, that time I did feel more than a tiny bit gleeful. Ethan didn't deserve Dad's attitude, but Max sort of did. He needed to be knocked down a peg or two, and George Harmon was just the person to do it.

Dad continued, "Last I checked, all of this started with you."

Max's head snapped back a smidge, but he was smart—or scared—enough to stay quiet.

"No, Dad." I went to him, taking him by the arms and shaking him a little until he looked at me. "This started when somebody decided to break into Ethan's house. It might even have started when they decided to kill Una for her money. We're not sure of that yet, but it's looking more likely every time this maniac decides to come after one of us."

"You know we'll keep her safe." Joe stepped up next to me and I couldn't have been more grateful, since his presence gave me a little more courage. For once, he was on my side against his mentor. "You can be there, I'll be there, we'll bring in a few others to keep watch on the store from across the street. The minute anybody goes near her, we'll have them."

"Dad, it's the only way. He has to feel like he's safe. Like he'll get away with it."

My father's eyes searched mine. "You would be willing to do this?"

"What's the alternative? I did my best to turn my back on this, I really did. Ask Ethan." Of course, Ethan looked like he would rather my father never ask him anything else for the rest of his life. "But it's too late for that. He knows who Ethan is. He followed us, he tried to force us into an accident. And we already know what he did to Brian."

I squeezed Dad's arms. "Dad. It's either this, or I'm looking over my shoulder every time I step out of my apartment. I know what I would rather do."

He could tell he was outnumbered. I felt it in the way his muscles loosened under my hands, the helpless little sigh he exhaled. "I'm going to be right there all the time."

"Of course. Though, you know, it might end up leading nowhere."

"I will sit in your office every day for the rest of my life if need be. You'll have a permanent security guard at the store." He wasn't kidding, either.

I tried to smile. "Hey, isn't it great that I at least told you about this in advance? I could've had Trixie run the story and then told you about it after the fact.

I think this shows remarkable character growth for me."

I could tell he didn't want to react, but he couldn't help it. His arms wound around me, pulling me in for a bear hug, and a begrudging laugh rumbled in his chest. "I swear, you girls are determined to send me to an early grave."

Emma made a disbelieving noise from her spot on the sofa. "What did I do? Why do you have to bring me into it?"

"Well, then. I'll turn the story in tonight. It'll be in the online edition tomorrow and the print edition the day after that." Trixie's eyes glowed with a light I'd come to recognize over the years. Sure, she loved me just as much as she would've loved a flesh-and-blood niece, but at heart she was a journalist. If she could write a story that would somehow break this case open, nobody was going to stop her. Not even my very gruff, very imposing father.

Before long Joe and Emma went home, convincing Dad to go with them rather than letting him stick around to harass me. He couldn't leave without a parting shot, of course. "You know, your mom's not going to be too happy when she finds out you arranged all of this without her knowing about it."

"Obviously, I'll let Trixie deal with her." I tapped the side of my head. "This isn't my first rodeo."

"So long as you stay safe in all of this." I couldn't miss the look he shot Ethan when he said it, as he was walking out the door. Was he a little miffed that Ethan had sped up rather than calling the police right away, when we knew we were in trouble? Probably—and I wished he wouldn't show it, since Ethan felt badly enough about it in the first place.

That left three of us. Ethan stood on the other side of the room, hands jammed in his pockets, his eyes on me. I didn't exactly hate the attention. I only wished we were alone.

Max cleared his throat. "I'll wait out on the porch." Though he made it a point to roll his eyes a little as he walked past on his way to the hall, because he couldn't resist the opportunity to let us know how he felt about the situation. Though even I wasn't quite sure how I felt about the situation, about the way Ethan looked at me as he crossed the room, about the tingling along the back of my neck which intensified the closer he came.

We stood together by the door, neither of us saying anything at first. I wasn't sure anything intelligible would've come from my lips if I tried. My tongue felt thick all of a sudden, my throat tight, my heart fluttering like a hummingbird.

He finally sighed, his brows drawn together. "I didn't want you to get involved in this. I hope you know that."

"I do."

"You have no idea how guilty I've felt since last night. I could've gotten us both killed, speeding up like I did. Who did I think I was? What did I think I was going to do?"

"Listen, if you hadn't done such a good job driving, we could've spun out. You protected us."

"I should've pulled over and called the police right away, the second I knew there was a threat." He still looked pained even as he reached out, his hand landing on my hair as gently as a butterfly. For such a grumpy, short-tempered guy, he had a surprisingly soft side.

"Surprise, surprise. When you're in a situation like that, you act purely on instinct. It's only after the fact that everything you could've done looks obvious."

"Why doesn't that make me feel any better?"

"How about this? I'm just fine. We both are."

He took a step closer, bringing to mind where we were before Max called and ruined everything. If he kept this up much longer, I would pass out—as it was,

I could hardly draw breath through my pursed lips. "Make me a promise?" He stroked my cheek with his thumb, his hand warm and comforting.

"Sure." Was he kidding? I would've promised anything.

"Let's keep it that way. You stay safe, and so will I."

"I'll do the best I can."

The ghost of a smile floated across his face. "I guess that's the best I can ask for." With that, he slid his hand around the back of my head, cradling it as he leaned in for the kiss stolen from us after dinner.

It was worth the wait.

"I'm starting to feel like an idiot." The store had been closed for an hour, after I'd ordered Becca to get the heck out of there. Sure, she wanted to be a heroine for Max's sake, but no way would I let her hang around in a situation like that. Neither would my father, who'd finally convinced her. He had a talent for that.

The lights still burned bright, the only business on the block open at this time on a Sunday night. It brought to mind one of those bug zappers, the light drawing all sorts of icky critters toward it.

We were waiting for an icky critter just then, too.

"If he saw the story, he'll come running." Pete was right. Trixie had gone above and beyond selling the fable we'd concocted. So what if I hadn't actually found the diary in the desk? There was no reason for Michael to know that. As far as he was concerned, I could've found it, flip through it, then put it back.

Pete's voice came through the earpiece tucked discreetly behind my hair. "I mean, if I were in this guy's shoes, I know that story would've scared me. If Trixie ever gets tired of journalism, she would be a great fiction writer."

"Gee, I don't know. She's never had much of a flair for drama." We both chuckled at that.

"Let's keep it quiet." That would be my father, who considered himself very much in charge of the situation. It was easier to take a step back and allow him to run the show.

I murmured an apology, glancing out the window and across the street to where Pete was waiting in a darkened car. He and Joe were both out there, while Dad waited in my office with the door closed. There were a few other cops wandering the block, keeping an eye out for anyone who looked suspicious.

Pete wasn't kidding when he said anybody would be scared after reading what she wrote. She'd made it sound like I had discovered some huge scandal in the pages of Una Howell's last diary, a diary which was now missing thanks to a burglar. She'd left just enough suspicion in her article, too, without coming straight out and linking what was in the diary to Una's suspicious death. There was a reason she'd worked for the paper as long as she had, even after all the hoopla when it changed hands and a lot of the staff was let go.

"And there's a car in front of Ethan's?" I couldn't help but ask, even when Pete was listening. Even though there was nothing between us, it still felt weird to mention another man in front of him.

"Don't worry. We have eyes on the house, and both he and Max are safe and sound." For once, Ethan was willing to avoid putting in extra hours at his shop in favor of protection. I hoped for all our sakes tonight would be the only time we had to do this.

The feeling of being a sitting duck wasn't exactly a thrill I wanted to repeat. Now that we were really in the thick of things, waiting to see if Michael would bite on the bait we'd set up for him, I wished we had never started any of this. All it took was remembering the white-knuckle terror of flying down the parkway with a would-be killer behind me to firm up my resolve. This had to be done.

"Heads up." There was an urgency in Joe's voice

that instantly brought goosebumps to my arms. "There's a pedestrian approaching from the east. This is the third time he's been around the block."

"I noticed him, too." Pete's voice was almost a growl. "He's not one of ours."

"Dark ball cap, dark clothes. Hands in his pockets, shoulders hunched." Joe paused. "He keeps looking ahead toward the store. Darcy?"

"Yes?" It took everything I had not to look across the street, to keep my eyes on the laptop in front of me and pretend nothing was out of order.

"You're safe. Remember that."

"Where is he, Joe?" I could almost hear Dad through the closed door and would've reminded him to keep his voice down, but I was way too anxious to think clearly.

"Three doors down. Two." I couldn't help but glance toward the window overlooking the darkened street. There were a few people walking around, but not nearly as many as there would be in the morning or afternoon now that so many of the shops in town closed earlier in the day than they normally would during the summer. It was easy to pick out the man Pete and Joe described as he walked past my store.

And instead of continuing, he stopped at the door. He tried the handle and found it locked.

"What do I do?" It was barely a whisper before I turned to look up like I was surprised anybody would try to come in at this time of night.

"Go to the door. We're coming, don't worry. Focus on him, not on us." Right. That was roughly as easy as peeling a turtle. Where had I heard that before? Some old movie from back in the day. Thoughts were ping-ponging around in my head, making no sense whatsoever as I walked around the counter and approached the door. The man standing on the other side of the glass was young, thin. Hadn't Ethan described him as being wiry? There was ice in my stomach as I reached for the lock, my trembling fingers closing around it.

The second it clicked, the man tried to force his way in, pushing against the door with both hands, throwing his entire weight behind him and knocking me back a few steps.

But he was too late. Somehow, Pete had made it out of his car and across the street without either of us noticing. "Police. Hands in the air." Behind me, my office door flew open, and Dad rushed out.

"You're okay. You're safe now." I walked into his embrace, shaking, weak with relief.

I heard the man protesting over the roaring in my head. "Wait, you got the wrong idea! I'm not trying to hurt anybody!"

Joe had joined them and was in the process of patting the guy down.

"You're not trying to hurt anybody? And why did you just try to strong-arm your way into the store?" Pete was practically snarling, looming over the shorter man. "It wouldn't be because you saw a certain story in the paper today and decided to pay a visit, would it?"

"You got the wrong idea. I swear." He lifted his head, showing me more of his face, his eyes locking on mine when he found them. "I'm not here to hurt you. I'm trying to warn you. You've got to be careful."

"That's what this is, my friend. Being careful." Joe retrieved a set of zip ties. "You're going to take a trip down to the police station and you're going to tell us everything."

The man's eyes never left mine, and I realized there was genuine fear in them before he cried out again. "You gotta be careful! I'm not the man you want!"

I stepped forward, ignoring Dad when he tried to hold me back. "Are you Michael Lewis?" I hardly needed to ask. I saw the resemblance to his grandmother right away. It was the eyes. They were just like hers.

His head bobbed up and down. "I'm telling you, he won't stop at anything to get what he wants. That's why I waited until now to come see you. I've been going around the block, making sure he wasn't watching before I came in."

"You wanted to make sure who wasn't watching?"

His lip curled in disgust. "The lawyer. Lawrence Bradley." He spat the words out like they were sour. "He framed me and sent me to prison to shut me up. What do you think he'll do you?"

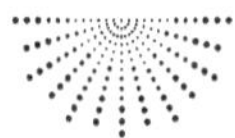

CHAPTER TWENTY-ONE

"Let's run through this again."

I watched through the two-way mirror as Joe paced in front of the table. Seated was Michael Lewis, Jr., whose knee hadn't stopped jogging up and down since the moment Joe put him in his chair. He radiated nervous energy, and I could understand why. This wasn't his first time in an interrogation room, and the last time he'd been in one hadn't ended very well. Not for him, anyway.

Joe stopped pacing, placing his palms on the table and leaning in. Even knowing him as well as I did, a shiver ran down my spine. He could be very intimidating what he wanted to be. "You saw the story in the paper and you went to Miss Harmon's store to warn her."

"That's right. How many times do I have to tell you?"

"Until it makes sense. What you're saying is, the person behind all of this is Una Howell's attorney, Lawrence Bradley."

"Attorney." Michael snickered in a knowing sort of way. "You keep calling him that. He was her boyfriend. For maybe six months or even a year before she died. They weren't exactly public about it, but everybody knew. It was gross."

"And how did you know, exactly?"

"For starters, the fact that he slept over in her room? More than once, even?" Another snicker, this one tinged with disgust. "Besides, Grandma knew about it, too. She didn't like it. She didn't like him. Any more than I did."

"And exactly how did you have this firsthand knowledge of what went on in the house? How did you know Mr. Bradley shared Miss Howell's room?"

"I saw with my own two eyes."

"What I'm asking you is, why were you at the house at all?"

I was no detective, but I knew where Joe's questioning was leading—and when Michael shifted in his chair, lowering his gaze, I knew Joe had the answer he was looking for. "Fine. You want to know? I would visit every couple of days. I was looking for money. But I would go to my grandma. I wouldn't take stuff from the house."

"So your grandmother gave you money?"

"Of course. She never turned me down. Una paid her well, and it wasn't like she had to pay rent or buy her own food or anything like that. All of her expenses were taken care of." He ran a hand over his black hair, which had been flattened by the cap he'd been wearing. "I'm not proud of myself, okay? I was a different person then. I was desperate."

"Desperate enough to get rid of the woman whom you knew had left your grandmother a small fortune?"

"No way. I would never do anything like that. Una was a good lady. She was like an aunt to me, and my grandma still talks about her all the time. They practically grew up together. I would never do that to her, or to anybody."

"Just like you didn't steal anything from the house, right? Even though that's what you went to prison for. Stealing priceless items and selling them for drug money."

"I'm telling you, I didn't take those things!"

"Then why were so many people willing to testify against you?"

"Why do you think? I'm telling you, it was all that

lawyer! He knew I was starting to get suspicious. He knew Grandma talked about him to me. I used to hear the two of them talking all the time, him and Una. It made me sick, the things he would say to her."

Joe straightened up, hands on his hips. He was intrigued—try as he might to hide it, I knew him well enough by then. "Such as what?"

"You know, romantic stuff. Telling her he loved her, talking about getting married." He pretended to gag. "I even asked her about it when I couldn't stay quiet anymore."

"And what did she say?"

"She laughed it off. She said she made it through her whole life without getting married, so why would she bother at her age." He shrugged. "I don't know. I believed her. But then he came in the room — I didn't know he was even in the house. I don't know whether he heard us or not, but he looked mad. He told me to leave, called me all sorts of names."

"What did Miss Howell do, if anything?"

His smile was grim. "She shouted him down. For an old lady, she had a pair of lungs." He chuckled at the memory, and anybody with eyes could tell he was fond of her. "She said something about people getting the wrong idea who owned the house. He went all wide-eyed, you know? Like he was shocked she would take my side."

"Did it end there?"

Michael's hands were on the table, and now they tightened into fists. "No. He said I was only there to get what I could."

"Weren't you?"

He flinched before sliding down in his chair. "I cared about her. What do I have to say to make you understand that?"

"Was that the last time you saw Mr. Bradley at the house?"

He nodded. "But he was still around, and he made sure to get back at me for that. I swear, I never took anything from the house. That's something even I wouldn't have done, no matter how desperate I was. I wasn't like him. I'm not that kind of person."

"What are you trying to say? Lawrence Bradley set you up?"

"Of course that's what I'm saying." Michael hit the table with his fists. "He took those things himself. He probably paid all those so-called witnesses. I knew them all, and I know they would've done anything for a little extra cash. It's not like we were friends. He set me up and sent me away so I couldn't get between him and what he wanted."

Then, his face crumpled. "And he made sure she hated me. Una. Grandma never believed it, but I think Una did. I never got the chance to tell her the truth. She died thinking I was a thief." There was a tremble in his voice. Was he a good enough liar to make this up and sound so convincing?

"I have to admit, the timeline doesn't quite add up for me." Joe turned away from him, pouring a glass of water. I saw what he was really doing, giving Michael a chance to compose himself before sliding the water his way.

Michael emptied half the glass by the time he was able to pull himself together. "It's pretty simple. I was already picked up and charged with the theft. Grandma posted bail for me. So I was out by the time Una died. That's why Grandma wasn't at the house that night. She went to my dad's, and the three of us talked about the charges and how things looked. Even she knew it didn't look good. We were there the whole night. I remember the last thing I said to Grandma before she left in the morning."

"What was that?" Was it just my imagination, or was Joe slightly kinder now?

"I told her to tell Una I was sorry, and to ask her to please believe me. Grandma said she would try. But I guess she never got the chance to do that, did she?"

I had almost forgotten my father was standing next to me. When he put a hand on my back, I jumped. "What are you thinking?"

"Honestly?" I stared through the glass, watching Michael's every move. "I believe him."

"What makes you say that?"

"He seems so sad. Almost heartbroken."

Dad sighed. "I'm almost inclined to agree with you."

Joe looked over a bunch of notes. "Did you ever know Miss Howell to take sleeping pills?"

"No, never." He was firm on this. "I mean, it might've made things easier for me if she kept prescription drugs around the house, if you know what I mean. But she never did. She never took anything stronger than aspirin. Something about somebody else in her family overdosing by accident or whatever."

I looked at Dad. "I've already heard that. Becca told me. He's not lying."

"And what kind of car do you drive?"

Michael snickered. "I don't even have a car."

"How do you get around?"

"The bus, mostly. Or I'll get an Uber if I have to." He looked up at the clock on the wall, his knee bouncing up and down harder than before. "I gotta call the halfway house. I'm going to miss curfew. If I do—"

"Don't worry about that. We'll get that all settled for you."

I turned away from the window, unable to listen anymore. Dad put an arm around my shoulders. "Are you okay?"

"If anything, I'm ashamed of myself. Of course, this guy's not driving a BMW. He just got out of prison, for heaven's sake. His family isn't wealthy. And he would be stupid to run all over the state, chasing after people he thought were a threat, when the threat of breaking parole is hanging over his head."

"Don't forget, though, people are capable of all kinds of things when they feel threatened. And if he had killed that lady and wanted to cover it up, he would be desperate."

I looked up at my father, trying to find answers. "What about a lawyer? What would he do?"

He took a deep breath and released it slowly before answering. "I have to admit, it's a pretty tall tale. But then again, it wouldn't be the first time somebody took advantage of an older person. And it definitely would not be the first time a younger man took advantage of an old, unmarried woman. Though from what I understand, everything's been on the up and up when it comes to the way he's managed the estate. And yes, we've asked around. He was very forthcoming."

My eyes bulged. "You spoke to him already?"

"Of course. It's an investigation. No, I didn't speak with him personally, but I reviewed the notes after the fact."

"So he's known all this time there was suspicion."

"Not suspicion. We were—"

"I know, I know. You were looking at the case from all angles."

He nodded. "That's right."

But that wasn't how a guilty man would see it. "And he went along with everything?"

"He's a lawyer. I'm sure he knows better than to withhold information."

Yes. A lawyer. An esteemed citizen. Meanwhile, somebody like Michael Lewis was seen as nothing more than a miserable addict—in recovery or not, it wouldn't make a difference in the eyes of so-called good people. It wouldn't have been difficult for Lawrence to set him up and get him out of the way. Maybe he hadn't planned on Julia being able to post bail. Maybe he assumed the family would turn their back on him.

"I wonder if Una wrote about it in her diary." I was looking at my father but I wasn't seeing him. I was back in the Howell house, imagining Una sitting at that desk, writing in her diary. "What if she had her doubts? What if she thought somebody had framed Michael? Or what if she was starting to doubt Lawrence? Maybe even both of those things."

"I'm sure that's possible, honey, but a million other things are possible, too."

"If he doesn't have a car, and he has to make curfew or else violate his probation, he couldn't have been the person who broke into Ethan's house. Just like it couldn't have been him following us the other night. And I doubt he was the one who ran Brian off the road."

"I think we can assume he's innocent of that."

"Which means he's telling the truth. So what about the odds of him telling the truth about Lawrence? It all adds up."

I had known him all my life, which meant I knew what it looked like when he wanted to disagree but didn't have a leg to stand on. "And he took a big risk, seeking you out. It could've meant heading back to prison." He said it slowly, grudgingly.

"Exactly, which tells me he believes everything he's saying."

"Well, we'll make sure he gets home and everything is ironed out." Dad took my face in his hands, something that always made me feel like a little girl again no matter how old I was. "Speaking of going home, you should get some rest."

No sooner had my mouth fallen open in surprise than he continued, reading my mind. "You won't be alone, of course. I've already made arrangements."

"Oh, really?"

"Don't make that face at me, young lady. Do you think I'd let you stay alone at a time like this?"

"I want to sleep in my own bed tonight."

"And you will." Something caught his attention and he looked over my shoulder. "Speak of the devil."

I turned slowly, dreading what I would find. "Pete. What a surprise." It was not a surprise.

"Hey. It's not like it's the first time I've had no choice but to sleep on your couch." He offered an apologetic grin. "But if you think there's anywhere else I'd be tonight, you're wrong."

CHAPTER TWENTY-TWO

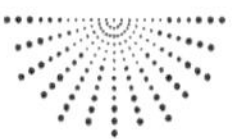

So. This wasn't like déjà vu at all. Having Pete stay over because a murderer was possibly after me was such a treat. What a delight.

I emptied my wine glass and wondered why I'd bothered using a glass at all. If this wasn't a straight-from-the-bottle situation, nothing was.

Pete finished his call with Joe, then came in from the side stairs. "Everything's fine with Michael."

"Good. He was only trying to do the right thing." I would've felt terrible otherwise.

He took off his holster, hanging it over the back of an armchair. It was a behavior so familiar, it almost made me cry. He could've been Dad twenty-five years earlier. "So you believe him, huh?"

"Sure. I absolutely do."

"It seems like Joe does, too." He jerked his chin, looking at the phone sitting next to me on the sofa. "Did you get in touch with Ethan?"

I wanted to ask why he sounded unhappy when he said Ethan's name, but I knew better. It was best to overlook it. "Yeah, and he knows to lay low the way he and Max have been doing. He said he can see the patrol car from his front window and everything's fine." Then I laughed. "Max is in heaven right now, going on and on about how this is going to make a fantastic book. Ethan wants to strangle him."

"That probably wouldn't be a good idea with the patrol car right outside." At least he sounded cheerful enough. "I swear. Even when you don't mean to get into trouble, trouble finds you."

"No kidding." I finished the sandwich I'd thrown together on returning from the station, one I had only eaten because Pete insisted. "Now, I don't know what I dread more. The thought of a crazy lawyer finding me, or what my mom's going to do when she finds out about this."

"She already knows about this."

I gasped.

He only shrugged it off. "Of course she does. She saw the story in the paper today, didn't she? Emma, Joe, and Trixie begged her to stay out of it until this is resolved. According to Joe, she was none too happy."

"Terrific. She's going to be furious and hurt."

"In the long run, she'll be happy you're okay."

"Sure, and she'll enjoy holding this over my head for the rest of my life."

"Well, we can't always please our parents."

He picked up the sandwich I made for him, which until now had sat untouched while he made his phone calls, and took a big bite.

"Please. You're the ultimate good boy. Don't tell me you know what it's like to disappoint your parents."

"I'll have you know they wanted me to go to medical school."

"You never told me that."

His head bobbed up and down as he chewed. "I was even pre-med for the first two years of college. Which was around a year-and-a-half longer than I wanted to be. I was determined to stick it out, though."

"What eventually changed your mind?"

"The fact that I was pretty sure I'd end up either burned out or catatonic or both if I didn't stop forcing myself through coursework that held no interest for me. I was surrounded by people with a passion for what they were doing. Really, truly competitive kids who wanted nothing more than to make it into the best medical school, determined to outdo each other. I remember wondering what was wrong with me that I didn't have that same fire in my belly."

This was news to me, the most he'd ever shared at once about his younger years. "Was it hard? Telling them you wanted to change your major?"

"Up until that point in my life, it was the hardest thing I ever had to do. But it was the right thing to do. I felt it." He put a hand over his chest. "As soon as I spoke up for myself, all the tightness I'd been carrying around in here sort of melted away. I didn't even know it was there until it was gone. So even though they were unhappy—and they were, extremely—all I had to do was go back to that feeling to remind myself I was doing the right thing."

"I wish I had that kind of courage."

He polished off his sandwich, raising an eyebrow before swallowing. "What are you telling me? Are you unhappy?"

"No! Not that way. I like where I am. I like who I am."

"I hope so, because I like who you are, too."

"But still. There are times I wish I could be brave."

"Like when?"

There was something about the intensity in his eyes that made my skin feel like it was too tight for my body. Not uncomfortable, per se, but different. Like something had gone and changed all over again without my knowing it.

Before I had the chance to speak, he shocked me by taking my hand. "I'm sorry. But all this talk about being brave… I have to say something." His fingers tightened around mine. "I can't pretend being with you means nothing. I can't act like I see you as nothing more than a friend. That's never been true. I don't want to make you uncomfortable, especially with us being in close quarters like this, but I had to get it off my chest."

Oh, boy. Funny how a few sentences could knock the world off its axis. Funny how I would've jumped for joy only a week or two earlier had Pete said those words. Like that night in the kitchen, flopping around in a pool of olive oil. That would've been perfect.

I realized he was waiting for me to say something. The intensity of his gaze was almost heavy, the twitching of his jaw revealing his nerves. What was there to say now? That he was too late? No, that wouldn't have been true. I still liked him a lot. That hadn't changed.

What had, then?

Simple. A second kiss from a certain grumpy-yet-charming baker who at that very minute was holed up with a weirdo cousin he still went out of his way for.

"Pete…" It felt like nothing I could say would be any good. Like I'd end up falling short no matter what. He deserved better than that—then again, hadn't he put me in this position?

Rather than allow me to continue, he shook his head. "Don't worry, you don't owe me anything. I had to get it off my chest. It occurs to me now that I could've picked a better time." He offered a sheepish smile. "I guess I was hoping for the best."

I squeezed his hand as tight as I could. "Things are so mixed-up again. It feels like we can't get our timing right, doesn't it?"

"That it does." He winked, giving my fingers one final squeeze before letting go. "I hope you don't mind me putting the TV on for a while. No way am I going to be able to fall asleep anytime soon."

"Are you kidding? I was going to ask if you'd mind me hanging out with you for a while, since I doubt I'll be sleeping. TV sounds good." My voice was too bright, almost shaking. Would we ever stop having these awkward moments? "I'm going to grab a shower if you don't mind. I want to wash the day off me."

"Good thinking. Take your time. I'll be right here." He leaned back against the cushions and picked up the remote. I couldn't shake a sense of guilt but told myself he was a big boy and could handle it. I could've turned him down flat, after all. I could've laughed at him—not that I ever would, of course. Things could've gone a lot worse.

And nobody ever told him to confess his feelings when there was no choice but for us to hang out together, either. That was on him. Just like it had been on me, trying to kiss him in a mad, impulsive moment.

Closing myself up in the bathroom came as a relief. I turned on the shower, drowning out the sound of the sports show he'd chosen.

"I hope you know we're watching something else when I'm out there!" His laughter told me he was well aware. At least he wasn't going to be a jerk about hogging the remote.

I took my time shampooing, conditioning, washing up. No amount of lavender-scented body wash would soothe my soul, not with Pete and Ethan going to war in my head. Was it slightly gratifying, knowing they both liked me? I'd be lying if I said it wasn't. That didn't mean I had to be happy about it, though.

In the end, I didn't want anyone to get hurt, especially not because of me. But eventually I would have to make a choice. Just then, the memory of Ethan's kiss was too fresh for me to brush it aside. That and how charming and romantic our date had been. The way my heart had just about ceased to beat when he'd stepped out of his car looking like a million bucks. The flowers and the special table and all of it, every last minute. I still felt all warm and fluttery inside when I thought about it.

By the time the water started cooling off without my touching the faucet, I knew it was time to get out of the shower. I couldn't hide in the bathroom forever. I turned off the water, laughing when I heard the same sports show playing out in the living room.

"Live it up while you can!"

He didn't answer. I figured he couldn't hear me over the roar of the crowd reacting to a touchdown or home run or whatever the heck was going on.

Once I was sure my robe was securely belted, I opened the bathroom door.

And found myself in the middle of a nightmare.

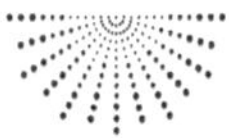

CHAPTER TWENTY-THREE

There was so much to take in all at once.

The open door leading out to the stairs.

The sight of Lawrence Bradley with a gun in his hand.

And Pete standing in front of me, his back to me, his hands up. "Get out now." I didn't think he was talking to Lawrence.

Lawrence who shook his head. "No, she's not going anywhere. Neither of you are." His eyes flickered away from Pete long enough to meet mine. "Some cop. He forgot to lock the door."

"Go." Pete was still staring at him but speaking to me. "Hurry." I didn't want to leave him, though. Not that I could've moved, anyway. Fear had me frozen in place.

Lawrence muttered a curse. "Do you have a problem with your hearing? I said she isn't going anywhere."

"The police already know all about you. This is a waste of time."

He only laughed, a cold and bitter sound. Nothing like the warmth and charm he'd fooled me with before. "Who are they really going to believe? Once I speak to them, they'll usher me out with apologies for wasting my time."

The memory of Michael's statement told me otherwise. "I wouldn't be so sure of that if I were you."

"But there's no proof, Miss Harmon." He almost looked disappointed. "You realize you made a major mistake when we first met. You thought you were so clever, lying your way into Julia's room, but the girl at the desk repeated your lies when she called me. There was no police investigation. Your father didn't work the case because I hired a private investigator."

I had forgotten all about that. He was onto me from the very beginning, twisting me up, telling Becca what he wanted us to believe. Knowing she'd spread his story about Michael, planting suspicion the way he'd planted suspicion in Una's mind.

"You hired a private investigator because you knew any detective worth the title would see right through what you did. Let me guess. You knew, or at least suspected Una was getting tired of you. What happened? Did she finally catch on?"

"Everything was fine until that useless addict started coming around for money. That little rat was always sniffing around, always where he shouldn't be. I should've gotten rid of him once and for all. I learned my lesson." He aimed the gun at me and Pete stepped between us to block him.

"This is a waste of time. Give it up now, and all you have is one murder to account for."

"What murder? There's no evidence of a murder. An old woman fell down the stairs one night." Lawrence laughed again, and there was something about it that screamed out his unhinged state. Granted, the gun in his hand did a pretty good job of that, too. "There's no proof. There's not even a diary anymore. I burned it."

"After you broke into Ethan's house."

"Honestly, that babbling idiot of a writer brought everything together for me. I would never have suspected the diary was in the desk if it hadn't been for him."

"The writer?" It was hard to latch onto any one thing he said with my thoughts swirling around in panic. "You mean Brian? Brian Mills?"

"He couldn't keep his mouth shut. He didn't even know who I was. All I did was ask why he cared about the desk, and he told me about the theory of Una's missing diary being hidden inside." He slapped his forehead with his free palm, laughing. "All that time, and it never occurred to me. If it hadn't been for him, I never would've known where to look."

If I lived through this, I would have to thank Brian for that. He could've told us about the man he talked to—then again, he probably never thought there was anything strange about their interaction. Lawrence could pretend to be the nicest, most reasonable person in the whole world when he put his mind to it.

I had to stall. We both did, otherwise there was no getting out of this. But Pete's holster was on the other side of the room, near the door. Lawrence was much closer to it than we were. "And you're the one who tried to run him down."

"I don't leave loose ends."

"But you did. He's alive and well."

He shrugged. "That can be fixed if need be."

"So now you're going to kill four people instead of just one? Oh, wait." The more I thought about it, the brighter the fury burned in my chest. "Ethan knows. So does Max. So does Becca, my assistant. And the woman who wrote the story in the paper. Michael

Lewis, of course. My brother-in-law who interrogated him tonight, my father who listened in. How many more people do you think you're going to get away with killing? This can't last."

"You'd be better leaving things the way they are now." Pete's voice was a lot softer than mine, more even. "One death, versus so many others. You'll never see the light of day if you kill us."

And Lawrence knew it. Yet he still stood there, the gun trembling slightly, sweat rolling down the side of his face. There were stains at his armpits, near his collar, telling me he'd been in this agitated state for a while. "I'll find another way. Nobody will believe the word of an ex-con over somebody like me. They didn't before, and they won't now."

"I wouldn't be so sure."

"Then let's test that theory, shall we?"

I knew it then. There was the slightest shift in his expression. His eyes went hard. Cold. Empty.

He was going to shoot us both.

It all happened so fast. No sooner did I come to that realization than Pete charged at him with a roar. A shot split the air. I screamed.

Pete crashed into Lawrence, the two of them tumbling to the floor.

"Darcy! Go!"

They struggled, fighting for the gun, while I cowered against the wall.

I knew I should go, but I couldn't leave. I couldn't abandon Pete. My head swung around, my brain struggling to come up with something while the men rolled on the floor. Lawrence's leg shot out, sending the armchair skidding out of place.

I ran for it, my feet moving before my thoughts could catch up. The holster was there, Pete's service revolver tucked inside. I unsnapped the safety strap and pulled the gun free. But there was no chance of getting a clear shot with the two of them tussling, growling and snarling and cursing each other with Lawrence's gun somewhere between them.

"Stop! I'll shoot!" I slid along the wall, aiming for Lawrence's head. "I mean it. I'll fire." The gun trembled slightly, but I steadied it, my eyes trained on him.

He looked up at me, seeing I wasn't kidding around. His face was red, slick with sweat, twisted in rage. "You don't have the guts."

"I do." Pete took Lawrence's wrist in one hand and pressed on the inside of his wrist. Like magic, he released the gun, howling like a wounded animal as he did.

He was beat, and he knew it. His wide, blazing eyes found mine. "Just do it. Please. Do it."

I gasped. "What?"

"Please. I can't… I won't…"

The wail of sirens filled the air, louder thanks to the door still being open. Somebody had called the police. He knew it was too late. Tears filled his eyes, spilling down the sides of his face when he closed them.

Pete sat up, still straddling Lawrence's now limp body. "No such luck. You won't get the quick, easy ending here." Footsteps pounded up the side stairs a moment before two uniformed officers burst into the apartment.

It was only then that I noticed what I'd missed up to that point. The blood spreading across Pete's polo shirt.

"No!" I put down the gun in favor of reaching for Pete, who only sat down on the floor rather than standing. "He hit you? I didn't think you got hit!"

He leaned against the coffee table, breathing heavy. His color wasn't great. Panic rose again in my chest. "He needs an ambulance!" I didn't know who I was shouting at. Nobody in particular.

"I'm okay." He didn't look or sound it. "Got me in the shoulder, is all. Would've… been able to take care of him… otherwise." He tried to smile but ended up somewhere closer to a grimace.

"Only you would charge at a man holding a gun." I brushed sweaty hair away from his forehead before pressing my lips against it.

He took my hand, holding on tight. "There's nobody I'd rather do it for. Though you could've at least run when I gave you the chance. Will you ever listen?"

"Will I ever listen? Last time I checked, you'd still be wrestling with that maniac if I hadn't grabbed your gun."

He laughed softly. "Okay. I'll forgive you for ignoring orders this time."

There was insistent banging on the front door. "Darcy? Are you okay in there?" It was Poppy, and now I knew who'd called the police. Poor thing. Living across the hall from me couldn't have been easy.

"Go ahead. I'll be fine." He squeezed my hand one more time before letting go, and a moment after I stood up, another officer took my place.

I went to the door and opened it to find Poppy wide-eyed and trembling.

Then I burst into tears.

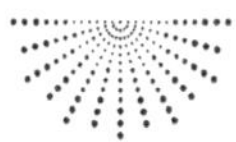

CHAPTER TWENTY-FOUR

"It's a flesh wound. He'll be up and about in no time." Joe slid me a reassuring look after ending the call to the hospital. "No worries."

I'd have to do my best not to worry, though it wouldn't be easy. The man had literally taken a bullet for me. How was I supposed to brush it off as no big deal?

Emma plopped her head on my shoulder. "Do me a favor?"

"Depends on the favor." As it turned out, I could still be sarcastic in the middle of the night.

"No more close calls."

The irony wasn't lost on me. How many times had I warned her to be careful? "I'll do my best."

"You'd better do more than that." Mom handed me

a cup of tea before sitting on my other side. "We'll talk about you keeping things from me some other time."

"Thank you. I don't think I could handle that tonight." I also couldn't handle being alone, though I hadn't expected so many people to come over. Becca had come on the run once I'd texted her. Ethan and Max had done the same once the officer watching Ethan's had told them they were in the clear. Dad hovered over all of us, never more than a few feet from me when he could help it.

I looked up at him. "Anything from the station?"

"You mean the station I'm not allowed inside while that… murderer is there?" He glanced at Mom, which struck me as funny. Like they were falling back into old patterns. She had always chided him for using salty language in front of us and he was still censoring himself in front of her.

"It's for the best." Joe withstood Dad's glare like a pro. "Trust me. It wouldn't help anything to have you there. It's why I'm here and not taking his statement." I noticed for the first time the way his hands kept clenching and unclenching.

"I'm okay. I really am." I tried to smile, tried to be as brave as I could, but in reality had only stopped crying maybe thirty seconds before everybody started coming in. Poor Poppy had endured the brunt of that.

Her shirt was soaked by the time I finished weeping on her shoulder.

Joe checked his phone again. "Texts from the station. Lawrence is spilling everything. The first smart move he made all night."

"And he seemed serious when he said he burned the diary?" Only Max would think to ask a question like that. Even Becca shook her head, eyes narrowed, but it was a little late for that.

"He did. Sorry." When Max's face fell, I took pity on him. "What does it matter? We know who killed Una and why he did it. Michael was right about him. So was Julia. And obviously, Una was starting to see through him, too. He couldn't let her drop him as her lawyer or her boyfriend."

"And these past few years, he's been living off the money she left him." Joe nodded when my eyebrows shot up. "We already knew that from our investigation. He never took on another client after Una. He didn't have to."

"So it was greed all along. How boring, huh?" I tried to be cheerful. I tried as hard as I could. Yet even I could hear how hollow my voice sounded.

"You're allowed to feel shaken up, you know." Emma rubbed my back, which struck me as funny since she was the pregnant lady. Wasn't she the one who should need her back rubbed?

"You'd know all about that." I winked at her and giggled when she rolled her eyes.

"Yes, so you should listen to me. I have experience with this sort of thing."

"And now, so do I. Unfortunately."

Mom looked at Dad, sighing dramatically. "Your daughters."

"Yours, too. They have a penchant for solving cases and are too stubborn to back down even when they should know better." Dad cracked a grin. "I'd say they're the perfect blend of the two of us."

Whoa. They were getting along. I exchanged a bewildered look with my sister, who'd frozen in place and spoke in a whisper. "I'm afraid to move. The spell might break."

"I heard that." Mom shrugged it off. "We might not have gotten along as a married couple, but the one thing that's never changed is how much we love you two."

Emma sniffled.

"Great. Now you've gotten her started again." I gave them both a disapproving look.

"It's just so beautiful." Her chin trembled, which of course drew Joe to her side. He was a tough detective, sure, but he turned into a puddle of mush when it came to his wife.

"Come on. Let's go home so you can get some rest." He helped her up—it seemed like her belly got bigger every day, meaning getting up from a seated position became more of a challenge all the time as the baby grew. I was starting to wonder whether the doctor was right about there only being one kid in there.

"I'd better get going, too." Becca glanced toward Max, who cleared his throat.

"I think I'll walk Becca home." When Ethan lifted an eyebrow, he did the same. "What?"

"Becca drove here." Poor Becca's cheeks went red at Ethan's observation.

"So he'll ride with her." She shot me a look of thanks and I winked in response. The girl had a lot of teasing ahead of her, but it could wait until we reopened the store in another day or two. I needed a little time to decompress, and so did she.

Besides, everybody would hear about this by morning and I doubted either of us would be up to answering dozens of questions.

Before they left, I had to ask. "Max? Are you still going to write about this?"

"Are you kidding? It has bestseller written all over it." Then he relented, dropping the pretentious attitude. "I talked with Brian earlier tonight, just to check in on him. We got to mulling over the idea of working together. I think this could go somewhere."

"I'm really glad." When he offered a patented smirk, I could only laugh. "Really, I am."

"And I really am glad you're okay." For maybe the first time, we exchanged a sincere smile. He wasn't so bad. Difficult, infuriating, sour-tempered. But not awful.

Dad checked the time. "I should get going, too." He eyed Ethan, his brow furrowing, and I wondered if he was waiting for Ethan to excuse himself. It hadn't happened yet and probably wouldn't until after everybody else had left.

Awkward.

Of all people, it was Mom who stepped in and saved the situation. "Come on, George. We're not as young as we used to be, and I have a café to open in the morning." Mom gave me a tight hug that almost brought tears to my eyes again, but I managed to maintain my composure for my parents' sakes.

Finally, it was just the two of us. "I'm pretty sure your father wants to find a reason to lock me up." Ethan mimed wiping sweat off his forehead.

"He's all bluster. Like somebody else I know."

"Cute." He eyed the closed door. "At least Becca got Max out of my hair."

"You mean you won't miss your roommate when he's gone?"

"Are you kidding? I'm already planning the party I'll throw after he goes home." He gestured to the sofa, brows lifting, and I nodded. The fact that he asked permission before sitting struck me as incredibly touching, like he wanted to make sure I wouldn't mind.

"You know, if they start dating, it'll mean seeing more of him around town." I tried to keep a straight face but couldn't manage it when Ethan flat-out growled.

"I wouldn't wish him on anybody. He's impossible to get along with, is in a bad mood most of the time—"

"Sounds like somebody I know."

"And now I regret telling you I like it when you give me a hard time." He put an arm around my shoulders and I leaned against him, glad for the contact when I was still so shaky.

"It's over now. No more looking over our shoulders."

"Do you think it would be safe for us to go out again? Maybe we'll keep it local this time so there's no chance of a car chase on the way home?"

I pouted. "Darn it. You know I'm addicted to excitement. Things are already getting boring between us."

I expected him to laugh or at least smirk, but he did neither. He took on a serious expression, almost pained. "There's a guy out there who threw himself in front of a gun for you. That's a big deal."

"He was doing his job."

"No. He wasn't." His sigh was heavy in spite of the light tone in his voice. I wondered which of the two represented what he was feeling. "I mean, he wasn't doing it out of professional duty. I'd put money on it."

"He was protecting a friend. And he did. Here I am, safe and sound." Hoping I was with another friend who'd come to his senses and understand this was hardly the time without my having to throw him out.

He waited a beat before smiling. "You're right. Safe and sound." With that, he turned on the TV and I settled in, my head on his shoulder, my legs pulled up next to me. It didn't matter what he put on. I needed to tune out, nothing more. Otherwise I might start thinking about the heart-stopping terror of noticing the blood on Pete's shirt and realizing where it had come from.

"You don't have to hang around." I yawned out of

nowhere—sleep was the furthest thing from my mind. "I know you have an early morning."

"Don't worry about it. I called my assistant and told her I wouldn't be in."

Wonders never ceased. "Ethan Crosby. That might be the most shocking thing I've heard tonight."

Whatever smart-aleck answer he came up with was wasted. I was asleep before he said a word. And when I woke up to find him snoring away, it was nice. I closed my eyes again, reminding myself I was safe.

Thanks to the man whose arm would be in a sling for a while. The man I couldn't help but think of as I fell asleep again.

For more Winnie Reed books click here!

Sign up for the newsletter to be notified of new releases.

Click on link for
Newsletter